TWO WOLVES
A CHARLIE STONE NOVEL

by

TREVOR TWOHIG

Two Wolves: A Charlie Stone Novel

www.trevortwohig.com
tjtwohig1@yahoo.co.uk

ISBN: 9798707131004

TWO WOLVES
A CHARLIE STONE NOVEL

by

TREVOR TWOHIG

1

Charlie looked out over Sunny Sands beach from the promenade as rage rose inside of him.

It was early evening and the beach was empty. The dark clouds descended over the stormy sea.

How could a place that had once brought him so much hope and joy now feel so alien to him? Had he never have found Amy Green's body in the wet sand, his life wouldn't be such a disaster now. Why couldn't he just have left it to the coastguard? Why didn't he just take his daughter, Maddie, for the ice cream first, rather than go rushing in?

Typical Charlie Stone, never able to leave things alone.

Gulls were descending on the beach, screeching their warning song, searching for scraps in their little gangs. The wind howled, causing sand, dirt and grit from the path to blow up in Charlie's face. He gripped the metal railing tighter. He felt the coldness and wished it would flow through his body up his arms, into his organs, into his heart and stop it beating.

His phone buzzed in his pocket. Charlie was annoyed that he'd even left his notifications on. He didn't want to be bothered. *People, too many people*. The cause of the pain. He just wanted to be left alone.

Eventually letting the comfort of the railing go, Charlie put one foot in front of the other and walked down the promenade. He stood at the corner of The Stade and contemplated his next move, more accurately he contemplated his next pub, The Mariner? The Ship?

The taste of whiskey was still at the back of his throat from the afternoon session he had just had, so he turned back and down the ramp and onto the beach.

His phone buzzed again, this time he took it out. Maybe it was Tara. Maybe it was Maddie.

'Yeah?'

'Hi Charlie, you OK? You sound rough.' It was the familiar voice of Charlie's DCI, Darren Jackson.

'Yeah, fine.'

'Where are you? It sounds horrendous out there,' Jackson continued.

Charlie looked up and noticed the clouds had formed and felt the first raindrop of the evening on his hand.

'Just out, you know.'

'Have you spoken to Tara?'

'She's not answering her phone, boss.'

'Have you left a message?'

'Yeah, three.'

'Good. Are you going to head home tonight? Back to Ashford?'

Technically, Charlie was registered as living with Tara in Willesborough, Ashford, but for the past three weeks, he had been living out of a small suitcase in the Grand Burstin Hotel in

Folkestone. Tara was pregnant and she didn't want the stress and 'bad vibes' of Charlie Stone around the house.

He didn't have the heart to tell his boss. Jackson had become a friend over time and Charlie didn't want him to know the full extent of his downfall.

'Yep, going soon.'

'Do that mate as the weather is coming in and you don't want to be stranded down here,' Jackson said. The rain was coming hard now, so Charlie pulled up the hoods to his gilet.

'Cool, sure.'

'You need to get your head back in the game, Charlie. Your leave ends this weekend, and I want you in bright and breezy on Monday morning. If you are serious about going after Troy Wood-'

'-Of course I'm serious! Why the hell wouldn't I be?' Charlie snapped.

'Well, you need to get yourself together. Stop drinking and get focused.'

'Thanks, boss. That's helpful,' Charlie said sarcastically.

'I know you've had a hard time of it lately, but you are bigger than this, you can resolve it.'

'Boss, I have to go. Speak soon.'

The rain fell harder and Charlie took shelter in one of the caves at the back of the beach.

Jackson meant well, but if he knew the half of what was really going on in Charlie's life, he probably would ease up a bit.

He held his head in his hands and tried to rid himself of the thoughts from his past that kept on coming. They just kept on coming.

Maddie on her bike, eating ice cream, smiling at him. But that was all gone now. He took out his phone and rang his daughter's number. It was hopeless as he knew that her mother, Jo, had blocked his number. He still rang though. Just in case.

After it failed to connect, he put the phone on the ground next to him, took off his shoes, socks and jacket and walked slowly and steadily towards the water.

The light was fading, and the beach was deserted due to the weather. Waves crashed, and the seafoam spattered Charlie's face as he continued walking deeper and deeper into the icy English Channel.

He smiled. *Take me away. It's too much. Take me away.*

When it was deep enough, Charlie began swimming, smashing his arms into the sea hitting the waves as hard as he could, kicking his legs ferociously.

I just want the pain to end. There was a gnawing, dull ache in his heart. It was getting worse. Time is a healer, they say. Not for Charlie, the pain was getting worse.

The sea rose higher, and soon the bitterness of strong liquor was replaced by the salt of the sea.

It was in his nostrils, in his mouth, in his eyes.

He continued pounding the ocean, seeking solace, seeking redemption until his arms couldn't swim anymore.

Maddie, I'm sorry. I'm sorry, I love you.

Charlie let the raging water carry him, as his world faded to darkness.

Finally, there was silence.

2

'He's OK. Yeah, he's fine. Yes, send him home? Sure, OK. Yep, no worries. See you later.'

Silence.

Charlie opened his eyes and immediately closed them again.

He recognised the bright, sterile lights of The Royal Victoria Hospital by Radnor Park, in Folkestone.

'Hi, Charlie. How's your head?'

Charlie knew the voice, it was the coastguard, Bill Edgar.

'Fine, I'm fine.' Charlie said, attempting to get up from the bed.

He felt Bill's hand gently push him back down to the surface. The rage rose up and Charlie took a deep breath. Bill's eyes were wide and filled with concern. Watery. Charlie wasn't interested.

'Just let me go, Bill.'

'Charlie, this shit has got to stop. One day I won't be on patrol and I won't find you out there. You will be a statistic, another idiot dead.'

The concern manifested itself as anger, like it so often does with men.

'I wish…' Charlie whispered under his breath.

'What was that?' Bill asked.

'Nothing. Sorry Bill, but I got it under control, that sea's tameable. One day, I'll make it all the way to France. What will you do then, eh?'

Charlie said sardonically.

'Not after the bloody skinful you had last night!' Bill pulled Charlie in close, 'this is some dangerous game you're playing. Rein it in, Charlie. I don't want to find your body out there.'

Charlie looked at Bill, but wasn't in the mood for lectures.

'OK, gotcha.'

Charlie got up and sat on the edge of the bed. He could see his clothes in the corner, and his phone. Good old Bill! But before he had a chance to make a beeline for them, the nurse appeared at the door.

'Mr Stone, good to see you awake,' she said smiling. She had a sweet smile and a slim figure, and for a moment, arousal knocked on the door. He wasn't used to it, having numbed his body with alcohol for the past few weeks.

'Yeah, feeling good as gold. Sorry about all of… this.' Charlie said, making it onto his feet, feeling sheepish.

'No Mr Stone, you must sit back and rest. You are lucky to be alive!' the nurse had a soothing African twang to her accent, and when she smiled at Charlie, he felt strangely comforted.

Charlie did as he was told and let the nurse take his blood pressure and his heart rate.

'Still beating?' he asked.

'Yes… strong heart, Mr Stone. Very good.'

Charlie nodded. It didn't feel very strong, it felt

broken. His family was gone, he had destroyed it.

'OK, you stay here and rest, OK?' the nurse said packing up her things and heading for the door.

'Sure.'

'If you need anything, ring the bell next to you. I'll bring you some water and breakfast.'

'OK.'

'The doctor will be coming around later to evaluate you, OK?'

Charlie smiled and pulled the sheet on the bed up, to make it seem like he was getting comfortable.

The nurse left the room followed by Bill who mumbled a goodbye, and Charlie got himself up, put on his clothes that were still rather damp, and waited until the coast was clear before opening the room door.

Charlie checked his watch. 10.34am.

He walked quietly along the corridor, trying not to alert anybody. He knew he only had a few more yards before he reached the safety of the double doors.

'Mr Stone? What are you doing? You cannot discharge yourself!' the soothing voice had become a threatening one.

'No! Of course not!' Charlie whipped around. 'I am just popping out for a cigarette.'

He said, his big smile coming in handy once again. The nurse smiled back and nodded.

There was an actual smoker outside the hospital

doors, so Charlie went and stood next to the old man, who was being held up by a silver zimmerframe.

'Hi,' he said.

The old man tried to talk, but Charlie was greeted with a grunt and a shifting of phlegm in the man's throat.

When Charlie was safe from the prying eyes of the nurse, he walked across Radnor Park towards the town.

He thought about getting a quick pint but it was too early to get served, he would have to wait.

He decided to head back to the Burstin and get sorted before moving back out.

Charlie felt OK now, like the exhilaration of last night had reset his emotional state. It wouldn't be long though until the demons came again.

Dark thoughts, never-ending dark thoughts, his new companions.

When Charlie got back to the Burstin it was busy with at least three or four groups in the outside seating area.

Sunday. Normal people meeting friends for drinks or taking the family out for a nice roast dinner.

Charlie shuddered, pulled up his hood and made his way inside the building.

In the lobby, he was greeted with the familiar, musty smell hitting him harder than usual.

He started up the stairs to the sixth floor, as he usually did as the lifts were often busy and he didn't want to wait.

Charlie liked the floor he was on, there was always something happening.

There was a prostitute working in the room three doors down. At night the door opened and closed every twenty minutes or so. Charlie would jump up from his bed and scope out the profiles of the men coming in and out, seeing if he recognised any.

This time as he made his way up the stairs, there were a pair of young men, smoking out of the window.

They looked Eastern European and when they heard Charlie come up the stairs, they looked at him aggressively.

Charlie smiled at them as he walked past.

They uttered something in their own language and Charlie laughed.

Go on lads, I dare you.

They didn't say or do anything, much to Charlie's chagrin, so he went to his door and let himself in.

The room stank of old socks and leftover food. He pulled the curtain and opened the window the sliver it was allowed to go. Perhaps it was for the best given his fluctuating state of mind.

Charlie showered and sprayed himself with some of the cheap deodorant he had bought at the corner shop on Tontine Street.

One more day, he thought to himself, and then he could get back to work and catch Troy Wood.

If it was the last thing he did, he wanted to make Troy suffer.

But he still had a good eighteen hours until then, and being alone, time always dragged.

He thought about calling Tara. Perhaps she was missing him. Perhaps she wanted to hear his voice. He checked his phone, no new messages or calls.

Fuck it.

Charlie grabbed his jacket and headed for the door.

3

'Yeah, I know. They're running away with it aren't they?' Charlie said to the barman, Nick, at the Ward's Hotel.

He got a cab up from the Burstin, as he knew it would be quiet at this time and didn't want to be amongst the norms, thronging the restaurants being social, doing what regular people do.

Charlie didn't feel like a regular person. He felt like a dog that had been beaten too much.

The barman placed a pint of lager in front of Charlie.

'Still, City will be a force next year...' the barman mused.

'United will be one to watch too,' Charlie suggested, looking across the bar and into the distance.

'What about your boys?' the barman said.

'The Hammers? We won't do anything. Not until those owners are gone.'

'You ended last season well though...'

Charlie was the only punter in the venue, besides a couple sitting at the far end of the bar.

There was a blonde, local girl who he had seen in and around the town before. She was pretty and had a lovely, friendly face when she smiled and laughed, but there was sadness in her eyes.

A broad, burly man, completely bald with eyes of steel escorted her.

He kept looking at Charlie, who didn't recognise

the man at all.

'… Some decent signings too…' Nick continued.

'Yeah, for sure. But there are too many big-time Charlies for us to do anything significant this year.'

'Big-time Charlie, eh? Just like you?' the barman smiled at me.

'No mate. Quite the opposite. The days of me being some sort of… I don't know…'

'…Hero… Charlie…'

'Don't be silly…' Charlie said, beginning to blush slightly.

'You are, Charlie. A bloody hero. You know you are…' the barman continued.

'Yeah right. A hero having his first pint before midday on a Sunday morning. Cheers!' Charlie said, tipping his drink and supping the foam from the top of his glass.

The bald man looked directly at him as Charlie put his pint back on the bar.

'All right pal, do you wanna come and join us?' he said.

Charlie looked over. He didn't really want to join them. He found situations like this uncomfortable. He didn't really want to third wheel this couple, who seemed to be on a date.

That said, the man didn't look like someone to be messed with and having no friends since Dave's death hadn't really been working for Charlie thus far.

'Yeah, come on!' the blonde, bubbly girl said,

smiling in Charlie's direction.

He was buoyed by her exuberance, joy and warmth. It reminded him of the girls he had lost, his fiancée and his daughter.

Charlie got his bar stool and scraped it along the marble floor to where the couple were sitting.

'Hi,' Charlie said tentatively.

'All right fella, I'm Robbie, but people call me Big Rob. This is Becky.'

Robbie had a gruff London accent, and had a habit of moving his whole body when he spoke, as if he were bobbing and weaving in a title fight.

'Nice to meet you.' Charlie said, taking a large gulp of his drink.

'I overheard you talking to Nick, and it's similar to us. We come in here 'cos we want to get away from the town, y'know?' he continued, looking deep into Charlie's eyes, searching for something.

'Yeah, yeah. I do know. It's a small town. Everyone thinks they know everyone.'

'It's a bloody nightmare. I hate it. I just want a quiet drink sometimes.' Robbie continued; Becky looked at him nervously.

Robbie's voice boomed; even when he whispered, the bass seemed to reverberate through the room.

'I know another little gaff in town that's just opened if you fancy joining us?' Robbie continued. 'It hasn't got all of the same divs in the regular places, it's a bit dearer, keeps the riff-raff out.'

'Oh yeah? What's it called?'

'Erm… hang on a minute it begins with a J… err… what was it babe?'

'Ain't it Junction something?' Becky added.

'Yeah, something like that. It's a good shout if you want to come down with us?' Robbie added.

'Sure, sure. Why not?' Charlie added. He was surprised he hadn't heard of the new place. Since he had been living in Ashford and on leave from the police, he was a little out of the loop.

'Here Char, I was gonna ask… where's your accent from, mate?' The lines on his forehead furrowing.

'South East London. Woolwich, initially.'

Robbie's face filled with joy and his eyes grew wider, 'I thought you was a London boy! I could tell!'

Robbie got off his seat and gave Charlie a big hug.

Charlie, for the first time since he could remember, forced a smile too.

The trio continued talking and learning about each other.

There was something warm and friendly about Robbie, yet he was guarded about aspects of his private life. Charlie was just enjoying some regular chitchat.

The drinks had been flowing rather quickly and it was his turn to buy a round.

'Here, shall we book a sherbet down to this Junction place?'

'Well, it's just in town, right? We can walk, no?' Charlie asked. He missed his regular walks with Tara. They cleared his head and helped him feel a bit more human.

Robbie smirked, 'Nah. I can't be walking about Char.'

Charlie nodded as Robbie had already got his phone out and headed to the door to make his call.

'Not big on exercise, your Robbie?' he asked Becky.

'Something like that. He has certain rules that he has to… it's better for him to be in cabs, put it that way.' Becky suddenly looked sheepish and snatched up her colourful drink, looking away.

'Right, let's get on our toes, cab's on its way.' Robbie boomed from the pub garden.

Robbie waited at the doorway and Charlie watched him look about from side to side.

Robbie's phone rang again and he picked it up immediately, partaking in a conversation entirely in monosyllables and grunts.

The cab arrived swiftly and took the three of them the very short distance to the top of town, dropping them at Cheriton Place, just up from the Escape Rooms and Sainsbury's.

The new bar looked fairly modern from the outside, with floor to ceiling windows and lots of greenery inside. The large white sign above the door read 'Junction 13.'

Robbie went in first as if to reconnoitre the place. He seemed happy that there was no-one in there he knew.

No such luck for Charlie however.

At the bar sipping a white wine was a lady from one of his favourite haunts down the harbour.

She smiled and he nodded at her. In his current state Charlie couldn't face small talk.

He felt awful and knew he was in a rut of drinking, darkness and depression, but the only thing that seemed to cure the pain was the thing that was killing him. So, Charlie stayed in the darkness and took another gulp of his beer.

The conversation with Rob and Becky had brought a brief crack of light… normality.

'I'll get the next round, Char. What you having?' Robbie asked.

Charlie looked at the selection and was relatively impressed. Different from a lot of the other places in town.

'Moretti, please.' Charlie said.

'Good choice, we are the only place in town that serves Moretti,' the barmaid said, smiling at him.

Charlie nodded.

She was a young, pretty girl, with dark hair and pale skin. Attractive, but not in an obvious way.

She was struggling with the gas and thus was unable to finish the Moretti off. Charlie could tell she was getting a little flustered.

'If you snap the handle back quickly, but keep

the nozzle under the foam it should help…'

She looked perplexed, so Charlie reached over the bar to show her.

She smiled, 'oh yeah!'

Robbie looked at Charlie with an eyebrow cocked.

'Misspent youth,' Charlie said, before taking his pint to a table in the corner.

Robbie paid, then he and Becky came over.

'What I like about this place is there are none of your usual faces in here. And, it's open plan so you can see what's going on.' Robbie said, taking the seat that faced outwards, towards the front door.

'Here this will be interesting…' Robbie continued.

The door opened, and in shuffled an old man. He was about five foot five inches and was wearing a cream overcoat and chino trousers.

He was shaking his head and looking perturbed.

'Oh hey, Phil!' the bar lady shouted across the room.

The man looked up at her and seemed confused.

He took a baseball cap from his head and went towards the bar. Suddenly, he seemed to have a change of heart, muttered something under his breath, and then he walked out of the front door again.

'He'll be back in a minute,' Becky said, sniggering to herself.

Robbie lowered his head and put his lips to his

pint and the room returned to normality.

Charlie caught the eye of the girl behind the bar who smiled, before picking up a mop and rinsing it into a bucket.

The door opened again and in bustled Phil once more.

'Here we go,' Robbie uttered, the bass of his voice reverberating.

Phil was red-faced, puffy and had tears in his eyes.

'What's up, Phil?' the bar lady said as he came up to the bar.

'It's her again. Her on the bleeding phone!' he said, through clenched teeth.

Although he seemed angry, it was clear that he wasn't typically aggressive.

'Who's that?' she asked.

Phil circled around. He was on edge, taking his hat off and putting it on again. Taking it off and slapping it on the bar.

'Drink, Phil?'

'In a minute, in a minute!' he said, flustered and living out some private drama in his head.

'Here, Char… remember Mr. Magoo?' Robbie asked, nodding towards the elderly man.

Charlie smiled and looked at Phil. He was the spitting image of the cartoon character from the 1980's. He must have alopecia, as there was not a hair on Phil's head or face.

He burst into laughter as Robbie looked on smiling.

'Stop it you two!' Becky said, trying to conceal her giggles too.

'What?' Robbie asked, looking at Becky and grinning.

Robbie then got up and went to the bar.

'All right Phil, how you doing?' he said and offered to buy the old man a drink.

Charlie watched Robbie confidently stride across the room, like an actor in his own personal movie, full of confidence, full of bravado.

The door opened again and Robbie shot a glance over his shoulder. He looked nervous, but then he saw who it was and relaxed, going back to making small talk with Phil and the barmaid.

'This guy is a funny one,' Becky whispered to Charlie.

'Oh yeah?'

He had tanned skin and black shoulder length hair. His square glasses and moustache made him look like an extra from some B-grade eighties movie.

He saw the barmaid, smiled and did a little dance. Robbie returned to the table with drinks.

'What the bloody hell was that?' Robbie whispered and again, they sniggered like school children.

She smiled back, but raised an eyebrow at the dubious dance.

'I think he only comes in 'cos he fancies Sharn,' Becky continued.

'Who's that?'

'The barmaid. She is a sweetie.' Becky said, smiling at her boyfriend and pointing at her drink, indicating she wanted a refill.

'Yeah, she reminds me of…' There it was that pain, the stab in the gut. Like a bullet it returned, crippling, horrible pain.

'Reminds you of who, Charlie?'

'Oh… no-one…. Erm…'

'No, go on,' Becky pushed.

'My… I have a daughter… a bit younger… but… yeah…' Sadness coming fast in waves, desire to kill increasing… rage intensifying…

'Oh, you have a daughter? That's lovely! How old…?'

Before Becky could finish, Charlie got up and took his phone out.

He waved it at her, as if to say he had an incoming call.

Everything seemed to be moving in slow motion.

Charlie was falling, drifting, darkness moving in, swallowing…

4

'Right, where we off to next, Charlie?' Robbie asked, his voice booming across the room.

They had been in Junction 13 for a few hours now. Charlie had instigated the shots of sambuca and vodka, whilst Robbie appropriated the bar's iPad and thus the music selection. Currently, there was an old school garage mix playing, while Robbie wiggled around the bar area, like a drunken bear.

Becky's face was a mix of drunken elation and trepidation as she watched her twenty stone boyfriend navigate the nuances of 'sweet like chocolate' with surprising aplomb.

'He's got some moves!' Charlie said, both of them sitting at the bar now. 'East Kent?'

'Yeah…' she said, continuing to look nervous, as Robbie boogied his way past Charlie and towards her chair.

He lifted her up as she giggled at him and they danced together, while Robbie belted out the lyrics, much to the enjoyment of the ten or so drinkers who had assembled in the bar throughout the afternoon.

Sharn was looking at her phone. She looked perplexed; her forehead scrunched up as she concentrated on what she was reading.

She noticed Charlie looking and immediately remembered where she was and smiled awkwardly, as if she'd been caught out.

'You OK?' he asked.

'Oh, yeah… just some weird article…'

'What's that then?'

'Oh, nothing, just that virus thing that's spreading. Have you heard about it?'

He immediately felt cold.

'No, do tell me about it?' Charlie said, pretending he had no idea what Sharn was talking about. He was interested in what other people's opinions were of the virus, since he wasn't entirely clear on his own.

Robbie's arse bumped a bar stool over, which knocked him and made him slightly unsteady.

'Come on son, have a little boogie!' he said to Charlie.

'I'm all right pal.'

Charlie looked at Sharn.

'It's just my mate who is really into conspiracies and stuff, has been going on about it for months, like literally months. Saying that the governments are all in on it, to release this virus which is literally going to kill loads and loads of people…'

'Oh yeah?'

'Yeah. And they want to make it look like it was an accident, so they have started it in China, and it now seems to be spreading, like a lot…'

Charlie felt sick.

He wanted to believe that Troy's words were just lies. That he was just boasting and goading. That the fact he predicted what was unfolding in front of Charlie's eyes was just coincidence. But yet, it seems Troy's plan was slowly coming to fruition.

Charlie nodded and looked away, back to the big, burly bear, bleary-eyed and blotto in front of him.

Charlie suddenly felt the need to leave quickly and get some fresh air.

'Robbie, I'm going to get out of here.' He finished his drink and walked to the door.

'Here, Char, wait up!'

Charlie took a deep breath, composed himself, checking the time on his watch.

7.23pm. About eleven hours until he was back at work, starting the new case.

He was tipsy. The cool, coastal air provided a wakeup call but one that highlighted he had drunk a little too much.

His life was disordered, but just when he thought he was clear, the darkness reared up and thrust it back down.

'Ere, Charlie? Fancy the East Kent? Let's have a sing-song at the karaoke, eh?' Robbie placed his big broad arm around Charlie's shoulder, his smiling face a few inches away.

Charlie couldn't help but smile.

The East Kent Arms was an intriguing establishment, slap bang in the centre of Folkestone's dilapidated high street.

Whilst the harbour area had witnessed a major, financial injection, central Folkestone had not.

The old Woolworth's sign was still visible above one of the many pound stores, which were flanked by empty properties, vape shops and an over-18s 'Cashino.'

That said, the East Kent Arms was packed.

It was the only place in town to get a late drink on a Sunday night and as such, the punters flocked.

They pushed open the old, wooden door and were greeted by a wave of warmth from inside the establishment. A middle-aged man in an open neck, white shirt that showed a bit too much chest hair was currently decimating a Johnny Cash song.

Charlie made his way through the throng and ordered three drinks.

There were some strange looks from some of the punters, whispers in hands and eyes darting across the room. They may have seen Charlie on the TV or in the local paper. Charlie Stone, the hero! The man who solved the Amy Green case.

Well, if one thing was true about this old town, heroes can become villains in the blink of an eye.

Charlie took a slug of his Guinness and waited for Robbie, who was currently nowhere to be seen.

He passed Becky her drink; she seemed anxious.

'This is what happens…' she said into the background noise of the pub.

'What?'

'This is what happens.' She said, directing the

words at him this time, 'the disappearing act.'

'Oh really? But he was so keen on coming here?' Charlie said.

She looked at Charlie and nodded, sharing the frustration.

Charlie shrugged, watching the changeover of singers. This time a middle-aged lady took to the stage. She had long blonde hair in curls and wore a white, silky dress. She was going to sing a Dolly Parton track. Bold choice, Charlie thought to himself.

'Where do you think he has gone?' Charlie leant down and spoke into Becky's ear.

She looked at him with a wry smile.

'Business.'

Charlie looked at her again, wide-eyed and surprised. Then it dawned on him. Robbie probably had no idea that he was a copper. Charlie certainly didn't present like one, half-cut in the pubs of Folkestone.

Becky's comment excited Charlie. That familiar flame rose in his gut and propelled him to investigate, to explore further.

'Just going to the toilet, Bex,' Charlie said. 'Can you watch my drink please?'

Becky nodded, but she was wrapped in her own microcosm of disappointment and disillusion.

Were there any men who didn't disappoint their other halves? Who came in when they were told and did precisely as they were asked?

Charlie went to the toilet, which was at the back

of the venue and noticed that there was some movement outside, in the makeshift concrete beer garden.

He finished and went to the door, opening it slowly.

Robbie was there talking quietly, yet animatedly, with someone Charlie did not recognise.

The man had dark brown hair and a ginger beard.

When Robbie saw Charlie, he exhaled deeply, like he was frustrated that he was there. Then he finished his sentence and smiled.

'Hey, Charlie. How's it going? I was just having a fag.' He said, grabbing him with both arms in a bear hug. He certainly was the affectionate type, despite being a bit of a bruiser.

The man with Robbie produced a wry smile and took a drag on his cigarette.

Robbie nodded at him and he dropped his butt and headed back indoors.

Charlie stood next to Robbie, the weight of the world on his shoulders. The Robbie that was dancing in the bar earlier, all smiles and cuddles, had gone.

'You all right, buddy?'

Robbie nodded.

'So, Rob, I wanted to ask. What is it exactly you do for work?' Charlie smiled, having a vague idea already.

He smiled back, 'drop it Char.'

'No, come on, let the dog see the rabbit, mate…'

Charlie had only known him an afternoon, but they had bonded quickly and he felt he could have a bit of fun with him.

'Listen…'

'Let me guess, you're in waste management and disposal, right?'

Robbie burst out laughing. Charlie didn't know whether he had seen The Sopranos, but clearly the joke was not lost.

'Yeah, something like that. I talk to people, yeah? Will that do?' he said quietly.

Robbie looked worried as if he was dealing with a serious matter. He was certainly not good at hiding his emotions when something was bothering him.

'Yeah, that will do. Now come have a drink. Your good lady is waiting for you inside.'

Three pints in and Robbie was becoming restless again.

He was like an irritable toddler, trying to hold in a tantrum. He had moved from pints to double Courvoisiers and the chance of a 'sing-song' now looked very unlikely.

'Hey, Robbie. It's been fun, but I'm going to make a move, I think,' Charlie said. Robbie looked frustrated; Becky exhaled loudly.

Robbie nodded slowly.

'How about one more stop, a night cap?'

'I don't think there are many places open now,' Charlie said.

Robbie laughed, 'don't worry about that son,

you're with me!' he said, a sinister look in his eye.

He downed his brown liquid in one go.

'Right, let's get on our toes.'

They walked down the deserted high street. It was now nearly eleven on a Sunday night.

'Mate, nowhere will be open now,' Charlie said.

'Trust me,' Robbie mumbled.

They were walking down the Old High Street and nearer the Burstin, so Charlie wasn't going to complain.

He had a text from Tara.

I miss you. Let's talk tomorrow. X

One kiss.

It was a far cry from the ten he used to get in their heyday, but still, it was a start.

Charlie wanted to be back home with her, but not in his current state. Not this… volatile.

'We're going in here,' Robbie stated, as they stood outside Gillespie's, which was all shut up.

'Hm, good luck buddy. It's closed,' Charlie said, as Robbie pulled out his phone and held it to his ear.

'Yeah, it's me. Two, yeah,' he said and placed the phone back in his pocket.

The door unlocked and slowly opened, revealing the bright red innards of the drinking hole, and around twenty different people, male and female, who all turned around to see who the newbies were.

'See, it's not what you know, mate, it's who you know,' Robbie stated, nodding at various shady characters, as he strode through the room, to the bar at the back.

'You're not wrong,' Charlie muttered, surprised, confused and somewhat impressed that he did not know that there were late drinks in his hometown, like speakeasies for the glitterati of the Folkestone underworld.

Charlie recognised some of the faces from the job, shifty looking fellows talking into phones, whispering behind their hands, eyeing him suspiciously.

Robbie nodded at the old man behind the bar in a Liverpool shirt, and the gent nodded back.

Robbie intimated to get three drinks, just as his phone rang and he headed towards the door.

He nodded at Charlie, suggesting he would be back shortly. The bar keeper mouthed the amount to him.

'You what, mate?'

'It's fifteen pounds, pal.'

'Yeah, I think Robbie is grabbing these ones,' Charlie returned.

'Robbie? Who's he, eh? He's not here!' the barkeeper sniggered to himself.

Charlie, not wanting to get himself involved in some form of conflict, nodded at the barman and took out his phone, tapping it on the handheld console.

'Thanks,' the barman said.

'No problem.'

Becky and Charlie waited anxiously for Robbie to return.

She smiled politely and made small talk, as she reapplied her lip gloss and checked her eyelashes.

She was stunning. But Charlie hadn't even scratched the surface of what her issues were with Robbie. There was certainly some form of dark side, it was written all over her face. She wasn't going to let on to a virtual stranger, though.

The time was nearing midnight. Charlie realised that it was unlikely he was going to get that drink he bought back from Robbie, so he decided to head to his room.

Becky decided she was going to get a cab back to her place and if Robbie turned up then great, but if he didn't, he didn't.

Charlie nodded in agreement and got up from his seat.

At the door, raised voices.

The door was shut, but Charlie could hear someone out the front, growing irate.

As the door opened Becky's face dropped.

'Oh, Jesus… Laura…' she said.

Charlie watched as Robbie stood shouting and pointing his finger into the face of the bouncer who was standing his ground, trying to keep his cool.

'Everything, all right?' Charlie waded in, trying to find his authoritative work voice, despite being well out of practice.

'You ain't got a right to pick her up and manhandle her. Fucking prick! Apologise to her now! No? I'll put you through the fucking window!'

'What the hell is going on?' Becky said, jumping in front of the bouncer.

'Leave it, babe. This fella needs to know he can't grab and intimidate women,' Robbie said.

'She's drunk and probably high, I need her out. Come on, you should understand,' the bouncer tried reasoning.

'There's ways and means though, son. And your way ain't right,' Robbie said.

'Get in the cab Becky. It is not worth getting into a fight. It's past midnight, now.' Charlie said.

Robbie mulled over his choices, walking from side to side, pulling a fag out of his packet.

Becky's cab pulled up along the kerb, totally oblivious to the atmosphere it would be inheriting.

'Listen, babe, you get indoors. I will meet you later. I need to cool down,' Robbie said.

Charlie looked at Becky who appeared dumbfounded. He gave her a brief hug and she got in the cab.

As Charlie turned around to find that his new pal had disappeared into the night.

5

Charlie headed back to the Burstin feeling buoyed.

Despite the somewhat abstract end to the evening, Charlie had found a friend.

He was moral and defending the honour of a woman and despite his flaws, it was clear he loved Becky in his own way.

Charlie also felt that his time in exile was coming to an end.

For Tara to text him and be forthcoming was a step in the right direction.

Charlie knew his behaviour in their house had grown erratic. He knew he was drinking too much. He hadn't taken the death of his best friend and mentor, Dave Woodward, well.

The banning order though was the final nail in the coffin. Listening to Maddie cry in the background, as Jo happily told him that he was not permitted by law to see his daughter, is something he would never forget.

That was what tipped the scales.

However, a good sleep, back to work and Charlie could feel that some semblance of normality may return. Exile would end and he would find the strength to fight and see his beautiful daughter once more.

As had become his habit when entering room 741 of the Burstin, Charlie turned on the sidelight and refilled his pint glass with tap water.

He brushed his teeth, avoiding his reflection in the mirror, turned out the bathroom light and put BBC News 24 on the TV as background noise.

As he went to turn the sound down, he noticed the breaking news banner across the bottom of the page.

'Pandemic sweeps across Asia with fears it has reached Western countries also.'

Started in China, now spreading across the globe… exactly as Troy had predicted in his letter to Charlie, a few months ago.

Charlie tentatively put his hand under the pillow and pulled out a small teddy bear. He was wearing a blue-striped t-shirt with a claret heart on it that read, 'Daddy loves you.'

It was the first teddy he bought his daughter when she was born. The first teddy she ever owned.

He turned the light out, clutching the bear, as tears welled in his eyes.

The light shone bright through the thin curtain and Charlie slowly came to. It was Monday morning and his watch read 7.12am.

For the first time in a long while, excitement filled him as he rose from bed and got changed into his gym clothes.

Grabbing a spare towel, his headphones and room key, Charlie went down to the gym and began walking on one of the treadmills.

He was in a strange dream-like state. His head was a little heavy due to the alcohol, like a patient stirring from a coma, ready to resume his life once more.

He got the running machine up to speed and pounded it as hard as he could. *Keep running, Charlie. Keep running. Leave it all behind.*

Sweat began to drip from his face and neck onto the dark grey plastic as his face became redder and redder in the mirror. Charlie sped up again, 16, 18, 20kph, his legs skipping and leaping, barely touching the mat beneath his feet.

Keep it going, Charlie, keep it going!

As the sweat poured from Charlie's frame, he smiled. The great purge, he thought to himself. Shed the skin, begin again.

Forty-five minutes later, after a sauna session and a swim, Charlie was upstairs putting on a new shirt and chinos.

He had treated himself two days ago, in anticipation of his return to work, not knowing where he might be staying.

He sprayed himself with aftershave and slicked his hair to the side with a small amount of wax.

He stood in the mirror and tried to raise his head to look at his reflection. His green eyes stared back. He hadn't wanted to look at his image recently, but he was pleasantly surprised at what he saw.

He took a deep breath and walked away.

He checked his watch, 8.23am.

Jackson wanted him in at nine, and it would surprise him for Charlie to be early, so he got his bag, room key and headed for the door.

Charlie took the lift as his legs were feeling a little sore from the exercise, and when he got to reception he made a point of nodding and smiling at the receptionist.

'Oh, sir…I think we have a message for you,' she said, turning away and leafing through a folder.

Charlie made his way over to the desk.

'Are you in 741? Charlie Stone?'

Charlie nodded.

'Here you go.'

He opened the note that was sealed in a peculiar pink envelope with a butterfly on the back.

Dear Char,

Was lovely to meet you yestaday and sorry I had to go off like I did.

I wud leave my number but I no our paths will cross soon enuff.

All right?

Ur new best m8

Rob.

Charlie smiled. He didn't remember telling Robbie he lived in the Burstin, or maybe he did? Anyway, it only added to Charlie's good mood as he made his way into the open arms of Folkestone. Yes, maybe Robbie was on the wrong side of the law and not Charlie's usual type of companion. Perhaps that was the appeal. Robbie was exciting, different… *alive.* Something Charlie hadn't felt for a while.

As he waited in Starbucks for his order, he remembered the text from Tara.

He immediately got out his phone and opened his messages.

Back at work, let's talk today. How are you? X x x

Tara was now seven months pregnant and Charlie had become anxious about her. He felt a wave of guilt and shame overcome him, that he hadn't been there for her, and had too many other problems. There he was, the good dog deep inside of him, trying to come out. Charlie wanted to pet him and welcome him home.

He grabbed his order and made his way further up the high street towards Folkestone police station.

By the time he had arrived his coffee cup was nearly empty, so after tipping the dregs into the kitchen sink, he refilled his cup from the pot.

He looked around at the office, busy with work even before 9 am.

There were some faces he hadn't seen before, as always, some colleagues whom he nodded and smiled at before heading up the two flights of stairs to his department.

He was immediately greeted by Karl, a solid DC who had supported him well on the Amy Green and Rosenkreutz cases.

As he walked towards the conference room, he noticed Jimmy sitting inside, playing on his phone.

'Ah, here he is!' Jimmy said getting up from his chair.

Charlie hugged his colleague. Again, Jimmy had assisted Charlie and Dave competently in previous cases, although Jimmy was a tad surlier and was getting frustrated that he hadn't been promoted to DS yet.

Charlie had tried to counsel him in the past, and explained that climbing the ladder only brings more admin, more bureaucracy, more irritation.

This is why Charlie had never taken the big seat, the DCI job. He didn't want it.

He could barely keep his life together, let alone look after the rest of the nick.

Jimmy was ambitious none the less.

'How you keeping?' Jimmy asked, looking up from the phone engulfed by his large, fleshy hands.

'Yeah,' Charlie thought about it. 'Been better, I guess.'

Jimmy nodded and understood. He looked

sheepish and didn't know what to say.

'And you?'

'Yeah, same I suppose.'

'Hm,' Charlie nodded at him and looked away.

Men; if only they could learn to talk about their problems a little more, it would help.

'You talked to Jackson about a promotion?' Charlie asked.

Jimmy scrunched up his face.

'Not yet. I mean, I listened to what you said and… things aren't great at home, so…'

'See how this case goes, eh? I am going to need a quality wingman, after that, who knows?'

Jimmy nodded and smiled at Charlie's compliment.

The men sat in silence.

Charlie turned around to see where the others were and noticed Jackson's frame leaning on the outside of the door. He had one hand on the doorknob outside, talking quietly to another copper whom Charlie didn't recognise.

Karl was standing behind Jackson too, waiting to enter. Karl hadn't changed in the five years Charlie had worked with him. He had black scruffy hair, a grey suit and designer stubble. He was taller than all the other guys in the department so spent a lot of his time bending over, looking a little awkward.

Jackson finally came in quietly shutting the door behind him and, with a shuffle of his papers, sat down at the head of the desk.

He smiled at the men equally, which surprised Charlie given he had been on leave for weeks now and they had spoken by phone, but not seen one another.

'Are we all OK? Yes? Good to see you all, and we have DS Stone back in the saddle. Feeling OK, Charlie?'

Charlie nodded.

'Right, so… what do we need to discuss here?' Jackson looked down at his papers, somewhat unprepared and a little flustered.

'Wood, sir.' Charlie said.

'Yes, yes. We will come onto that…'

Charlie took a sharp intake of breath, feeling the rage rise. Getting Troy Wood is all that had been keeping him going through these dark times…

'There was a case of the lad with a hatchet in his leg. Karl, do you want to run us through that?' Jackson asked.

Charlie waited patiently, making notes reticently on the misdemeanours and various crimes that had been dealt with over the past few weeks.

'OK… if all that's taken care of let's talk about the Wood case.'

Charlie shifted in his seat.

'What have we got? The book that Charlie gave us after the Rosenkreutz-Green case…' Jackson said, jotting down some notes.

Charlie wondered what he could possibly be writing down at this stage?

'Erm… Charlie… anything else?'

'Yes… before my leave I emailed out the letter that Tara and I received at our new home from him…'

'Well, believed to be from him…' Jackson corrected.

Charlie shot him a warning glance and Jackson looked back down at his papers.

'Now, no-one outside of this police force should have known where my new address was. He also managed to find me when I was in police protection in Dover. So-'

'-So, we shouldn't jump to any conclusions, Charlie. I mean, he certainly has it in for you, that's no secret. We also need to make sure that we source where this possible leak is coming from…' Jackson interjected.

'Leak?' Jimmy added.

'How else could he know this information?' Jackson asked.

'I don't know… but we know that he has become incredibly powerful and gained even more powerful friends. Maybe he's watching all of the time…'

'Potentially. Either way, it needs to be sorted out,' Charlie said bluntly.

Since Dave had gone, there was no one Charlie fully trusted and if Troy was not the omnipotent force he professed to be, then he must have an ally in Charlie's department, a rat, who was risking the safety of Charlie's family.

'As far as I can tell, Wood is done with me.'

Charlie said.

'Oh yeah?' Jimmy replied.

'Yeah. I haven't been at home. Tara has been there, pregnant and alone. I have CCTV in the house,' Jimmy looked at Jackson and raised an eyebrow.

Jackson's brow furrowed.

'If he wanted to really get at me, this would have been his time. He hasn't. Did everyone read the letter he sent?' Charlie asked, attempting eye contact with the men around the table.

Jackson nodded while Karl and Jimmy both opened their phones, suggesting they had not. Charlie pressed on regardless.

'That email suggests he is on to bigger, more dangerous, more crippling things. Even to the extent of bringing this country to its knees.'

Karl looked at Jimmy and gave him a wry smile.

'If you had read the letter, you would know what I mean.' Charlie said, putting the DC in his place.

Karl stopped smiling and read the letter on his phone.

'What he says he is going to do, is happening right now.' Charlie continued.

'This thing started as a local sex circle for old men who wanted to get with young girls, but what we have learnt is that there is far more to it than that. These guys are connected to one another; Wadham, Wood, Green. And they are powerful. It goes all the way to the top of the chain.'

'Steady on, Charlie!' Jackson interjected.

'Turn the news on, skip.' Charlie returned.

Jackson reticently reached for the remote and turned on the flat-screen projector.

'Further to the story we broke earlier this week, the global pandemic is growing throughout south-east Asia, with thousands of cases being confirmed...'

'But why?' Karl asked. 'Why does Troy Wood want to do this?'

'Good question,' Charlie returned, in his flow, feeling like he was returning to somewhere near normality. 'I am not sure that he is entirely in control of what is happening. In fact, I would suggest he hasn't been the whole way through this journey. First it was Wadham, then Rosenkreutz and Jenny Green pulling the strings. In his aggressive ascent to the top, I think he is just another pawn in a bigger, more complex game.'

'So, if in effect he is just bait, why go after him? Why not find out who the "top boys" are?' Jimmy suggested.

Charlie stared at him from across the table.

'Is that a serious question, Jim?'

'Well, I mean-'

'-Let's have it right. This guy had a serious hand in the murder of Amy Green. He is connected to 'The Order.' Remember, these weren't some idiots working out of a garage. It was a heavily - funded, heavily-armed operation. He was involved in all of those deaths, brutal deaths of kids. He could have stopped it. And, indirectly he is responsible for the death of a police officer…'

'Not to mention the effect his actions have had in the lives of people around us…' Jackson nodded at Charlie as he spoke. He knew this was personal.

'I think the issue we have is how do we pin any of this on him?' Jackson continued.

'Well, we have Troy's book, 'Original Sin,' and his letter, which shows intent and has got to be brought forward as some form of confession…' Charlie stated.

'Hm…. But actual evidence of him committing…'

'…Look, I have had him in custody before and I broke him then. I can break him again, no matter how big or clever he thinks he is.'

There was a pause.

'The good news is that there is a small budget allocated to this. Charlie, I'm guessing you want to lead the case?'

Charlie nodded.

'OK. Jimmy, you can assist DS Stone too. Where are you going to start, if I may ask?' Jackson said.

'Got a few leads, skip. I may pay our old friend Paul Wadham a visit in Wakefield first. Then there are some companies I believe he is attached to in London.'

'OK, good stuff. Is there anything else lads?' Jackson said, pulling his papers together.

The room was quiet and the men began to raise themselves from their chairs.

'Well, if that's all, let's get to work.'

6

The policemen filtered out and Karl took Charlie to a standalone desk.

'That's you, mate.' Karl said.

'No problem.'

He sat down and fired up the old computer.

He had started making notes over the weekend of areas he needed to look into regarding this case.

During his leave he had analysed Troy's book to see if he could glean any further clues at all.

The book itself was made with top quality materials: high grade parchment paper, velvet hardback cover with gold embossed writing.

It was difficult to find out where Troy would even have had it made as it was so ornate and antique in style.

It would appear that Wood's plan of becoming an established author was just a ruse. He really wanted to write a solitary memoir, or was it a foretelling of the future? He did suggest that the world would be crippled and he would be the architect. Charlie felt cold, thinking about it. Either way, Troy's memoir was just for the eyes of Charlie Stone; so it was Charlie who needed to stop him.

In addition, there was not a fingerprint or a company name, anything at all for Charlie to go on. He deliberated about putting an ad out for high-quality book printing but knew this wouldn't narrow the search. What Troy had produced was something incredibly niche and if he had paid someone to do it, Charlie was sure he had paid them enough to keep quiet about it.

Then there was the letter.

Again, there were no discerning features. It had the same gilt-edges as the book, but in essence was just a note in an envelope.

Charlie looked at the letter he had saved on the police system:

'In six weeks, the world will be unrecognisable: panic, fear and death...'

It was five weeks since that letter had been received and Troy's promise was beginning to come true.

Charlie cross-referenced Troy Wood's name with two companies that he believed him to be affiliated with.

One was called Thraxin, a large pharmaceutical multi-national, based in north-west Kent. The other was a media company based in London, called Wolfire. He bookmarked both sites so he could research them in more detail later.

Coffee called. Charlie went back to the communal kitchen, checking his phone on the way. He had two texts, both from Tara:

Glad you are back at work. Good luck! X X X

Let me know when you go for lunch X X X

The texts were a bit of a surprise as it would seem Tara had a wholesale change of heart. The fire still burned in him to make it work. He yearned for her presence, her love, her approval. Checking his watch, he was surprised to find that it was coming up for 11.30am already.

I reckon 1pm for lunch X

He was glad that Tara wanted to speak to him, and guessed she would call sometime after one o' clock.

He put two sugars into his black coffee and went back to his desk, determined to find a substantial opening to what he could now call 'The Troy Wood case.'

The man had remained particularly elusive and slippery up to this point, so he knew that it was going to be a challenge, a challenge Charlie was very much up to. In fact, it was fair to say, since Charlie's conversation with him after his talk in the Best Western, he had largely disappeared from the face of the earth.

Back at his desk Charlie made notes regarding the structure and setup of the two businesses in question, he made a mental note to check in with Jimmy.

He was a great copper but had the potential to be temperamental. He needed a bit of management, an arm around the shoulder, to be told he was doing a good job. Not dissimilar to Charlie in his younger years. In fact, who was he kidding? He still needed it now!

Time passed swiftly and one pm arrived.

Charlie knew there was little to no phone reception on the second floor, so he got his jacket and went downstairs and out onto Bouverie Road West to await Tara's call.

As he came downstairs and out into the brightness of the afternoon, he saw Tara standing on the pavement looking towards him.

He smiled and she smiled back, holding her belly that was protruding now with the weight of their first child.

'Hi!' Charlie said eagerly.

'Well, hello, Detective Stone,' Tara returned, as Charlie came closer.

'What a pleasant surprise...' Charlie continued, nervously.

'Well, I was in the area. Don't get ahead of yourself,' she said, smiling coyly.

'I see...'

'So, where are you taking me?'

'I'll take you anywhere you want to go,' Charlie said, reciting one of his favourite song lyrics.

Tara smiled.

'Let's see if The Tavernetta is open.'

The upmarket environment immediately made Charlie nervous. He could tell that Tara was too. He waited to see what she wanted to say.

They were given the two-course lunch menu, Tara ordering a lemonade and Charlie a sparkling water.

'This takes me back to one of our first dates,' Charlie said tentatively.

'That's why I wanted to come here. It holds good memories for us, when things were less... stressful.'

'Hm.' Charlie agreed. He was like an oyster, closed up, not yet willing to be prised open for the world to get at once more.

'It's been tough on you, Charlie. I do see that.' Tara said, placing her hand in his.

Charlie looked away as Tara continued.

'I hope you understand that I never wanted us to separate at all. That night when you came back and you-'

'-I remember what I did, T...'

'... And I'm not trying to make you feel bad... but I had to protect us and the baby Charlie. I was scared and probably should have done things differently...'

The waiter came with the starters and placed them gently in front of them. Charlie had lost his appetite somewhat, but Tara tucked in.

'That night, I wasn't me. I lost control...I...it felt like someone had taken over me, rampaging…'

'Listen to me.' Tara interrupted. 'You can tell me as much as you like that you were grieving and you were drunk and so on. Until you face the truth, we can never move forward.' Tara said, looking deeply into Charlie's eyes.

'What do you mean?'

'Listen, I love you and I do think Dave's death has hurt you deeply, and I know in some way you blame yourself...'

Charlie winced at her words.

'... But what you're hiding is guilt and shame over losing Maddie. You blame yourself that you can't see her-'

'-I don't want to talk about this-'

'-You miss her and you're suppressing your rage about it...'

'... Tara, seriously...'

'... And you don't want to talk about it because Jo has convinced you that you are a bad father and you have let Maddie down...'

'...Please...' Charlie looked away, his red face was a confusion of emotions, tears were forming in his eyes.

'Look at me, Charlie. You need to fight for her and you need to get her back. You are strong enough to do this.'

Charlie looked at Tara and nodded unconvincingly.

'I want you to come back, Charlie. I need you; my unborn baby needs you but, most of all, Maddie needs you.'

'She won't let me see her...' Charlie said.

'Well, then you need to fight her. We need to fight her. Through the courts, if necessary. You can't let these people, Jo and Troy, take your family away from you.'

Charlie collected his thoughts and took a moment to steel himself before replying.

He wasn't used to feeling supported like this. Sure, he had friends like Dave who had been there for him, but not like this.

'OK, you're right. I love you, Tara. Let's make it right with us,' Charlie said, leaning over and kissing her on the lips.

'And get our family back,' Tara said, holding Charlie's face.

'Yes,' Charlie whispered.

They stared at one another across the table.

Tara was crying, smiling. The rest of the world had fallen away and for a brief moment, it was just the two of them and nothing else mattered.

7

Tara and Charlie finished their lunch and walked back to Folkestone police station.

'So, will I see you later tonight?' Tara asked.

'Yes, definitely. Just need to get my stuff from the hotel and then I'll head back. If that's what you want?'

'OK, don't be too late.' Tara said, kissing him, then walking back towards the town.

Charlie was in a dream state. Maybe life would be OK after all, maybe that dull ache of dissatisfaction would finally disappear.

For good.

Despite his newfound joie de vivre, he had work to do. Tomorrow he would need to start on the Wood case, so any final preparations had to be made today.

Back at his desk, he fired up the old computer.

'Hey, Charlie?' A voice came from behind him. It was Jimmy.

'Hey, Jim! I need to catch up with you actually, take a seat.'

'Yeah, sure. Did you see the gaffer?'

'No, why's that?' Charlie asked.

'Oh, I think he wanted to see you.'

Charlie looked over to Jackson's office. His blinds were closed which normally meant he was busy.

'Urgent?' Charlie asked.

Jimmy nodded.

'Right. Hold that thought.' Charlie said, getting up from his chair and heading towards Jackson's door.

He knocked lightly.

'Yes?'

Charlie opened the door slightly and looked into the darkness.

Jackson flicked on his desk lamp.

'Charlie, come in.'

'Are you all right in here boss? A bit... dark...' Charlie said, taking a seat opposite his boss.

Jackson swung from side to side on his chair and rubbed his eyes.

'What's the matter?' Charlie became anxious, sensing the mood.

'Did I see you with Tara earlier?' he said.

'Yeah, why?' Charlie asked defensively, shifting in his seat.

'Good, just wondering Charlie. Things getting better? I could tell there was something going on... I knew you weren't staying there...'

'Once a detective, eh boss? What's with the small talk, anyway? What's going on?'

Jackson exhaled deeply.

'Charlie, every case as you know, now needs to be signed off by the Super, especially as budgets are tighter than ever. The bosses are crapping themselves about this virus and can see money being needed as the country could potentially be locked down...'

'OK, so...?'

'We… I mean, I took the Wood case to him and said we need to finish this off and get the bastard who was still answerable for all of the crimes we discussed earlier-'

'-And let me guess, the budget's been cut for the Wood case, "in the current climate?"' Charlie said sarcastically.

'Yes, Charlie. But actually, there is erm… no budget for this case, it has been thrown out completely…'

'What?'

'Super doesn't want this Troy Wood case to go forward at all. I'm sorry to tell you this, Charlie, it's dead in the water.'

Charlie's brow furrowed and he let out a wry smile.

'Is this why you're sitting in darkness?'

'It's been a stressful day. I know how much this case means… would have meant to you. I know it's personal on a number of levels. You deserve to get this guy.'

'So, what's the reason behind this then?'

Jackson shrugged.

'Your guess is as good as mine.'

'Don't give me that! You know why. Don't try and bullshit me, Jacko.'

Jackson paused, thinking carefully about his next words.

'Some cases, Charlie…' he stopped and Charlie waited. 'Some cases are untouchable. That's it. This is a no-go under any circumstances. That was the message.'

'That's that?'

'That, I am afraid, is that.' Jackson confirmed.

Charlie nodded and thought about everything that had happened over the past year and a half, about the deaths of Amy Green and her best friend, Mina Burrows. He thought about Lucia and all of the kids tortured and murdered by the Order. He thought about Paul Wadham who was still alive. He thought about Dave Woodward who was not.

'Charlie, I want you to take some time…' Jackson started, but Charlie raised his hand to stop him.

He took his badge from his trouser pocket and he placed it on the desk.

'That's it, I'm out. For good.'

'Charlie, whether you are a copper or not, you can't go after this guy…'

'Ha! Oh really?' Charlie smiled. 'I thought you knew me better.'

'You have a notice period, Charlie. Don't throw away a good career, a good pension…'

'Fuck that, Darren. I'm out. You have been good to me, but you know me better than that. It's not personal, I like you. But I can't do this anymore. It's bullshit.'

Jackson looked at his maverick, his diamond in the rough and contemplated what to say to him. He settled on nothing.

Nodding, he stood up as Charlie did. The two

men embraced.

'I'm sorry, buddy,' Jackson said.

Charlie believed him. He nodded.

'It's OK. See you around.'

8

Freedom was a whisper away.

It sat perched on Charlie's shoulders like a fledgeling; unsteady, excited.

The unknown ahead of him, the comfort of all he had learnt behind him, Charlie headed out into his own brave new world.

His first stop was going to be Ward's Hotel to collect his thoughts.

He dragged his feet up the concrete steps that led up to the old, wooden doors. The familiar sound of the bell upon entrance, the receptionist who smiled and waved at Charlie, and around the left-hand corner into the glory of his sanctuary.

'Well, well, well! What are the odds, eh?' Robbie had a broad grin across his face as Charlie headed into that warm, welcome bear hug.

'Good to see you again. Drink?' Charlie asked.

'Yes mate, lager please.' Robbie said, heaving his heavy frame back onto the bar stool.

Charlie ordered drinks and sat with his new-found pal. Robbie looked at him, smiling.

'What's up? Something funny?' Charlie said smiling back.

'You got something to get off your chest, bro. I can tell.' Robbie said, shifting in his seat.

He was an astute man. It was as if he was reading Charlie's mind. He guessed it must have been his 'line of work,' living on your toes and learning to read people, what they will do, how they will react, that made him such a good judge of character.

'Funny you should say that, I just left the force.' Charlie answered.

'No shit? Really?' Robbie replied. The barman who was pouring the drinks, looked up at Charlie.

'Yeah. It's just… I've had enough. It's too corrupt.'

'Like any organisation, fella. Eventually it always turns. What's happened?'

'This case I wanted. You know the Troy Wood one…' Charlie stopped, realising Robbie probably didn't know about this.

'Oh right, yeah…' he said, kindly, keeping the conversation rolling.

'Well, they have chopped it. It's gone. No budget.'

'Oh… sorry to hear that…' Robbie said.

'The thing is Rob, this guy he…' Charlie took a deep breath. '…he is the reason that those girls died last year…'

'What? The girl on Sunny Sands?'

Charlie nodded tentatively, looking down at the floor.

'He's the reason that I'm not seeing my little girl-'

'Oh, really?' Robbie said loudly. 'Well, we know what we need to do then, don't we?' Robbie said, taking a drink from his pint glass.

Charlie looked up.

'We need to go and sort this guy out, don't we, Char?'

Charlie couldn't help but smile.

'Robbie, this isn't some hoodlum, some tearaway-'

'-I know that, son. What do you think I am? All I am saying is, you're my pal. And my line of work is... bringing certain people into line, if you know what I mean. So, this is just an extension of that, if you ask me.' Robbie concurred.

'Well, of course I don't entirely know what your line of work is Robbie...' Charlie said, tongue firmly in cheek, fishing for more details.

Robbie sighed, but he had a sly smile on his face.

'Listen Char, what can I say? Let me put it this way. Let's assume we go into business and we sell Tango, right? We obviously need distributors to make sure they get the Tango out to all of the people we need it to get to, yeah? But what if, say, some smart cunt thinks he can sell his own version of Tango and it isn't as good? That isn't right, is it? I've got to make sure that person stays in line and sells our Tango. Make sense?'

Charlie was surprised by Robbie's admission. He was an enforcer.

He looked at Charlie with his serious eyes, baby blue.

'That's not for everyone to know, right?' It was a

warning rather than a request. 'Plus, I'm trusting you, Charlie. As a friend, not a rozzer.'

Charlie nodded.

'So, when do you want to start?' Robbie asked.

'I've got to get back to Ashford tonight, but since I have no plans to go back to the bureaucracy of the force any time soon, fuck it, why not?'

'Nice one. You going back to see the missus, tonight?'

'Yeah, we had lunch today. Going to give things a go,' Charlie said sheepishly.

'Nice one! Listen, you get the beers in, I'll make a few phone calls and we can sort out what we're doing tomorrow, yeah?' Robbie said, getting from his stool and heading to the front garden.

Charlie turned to the bar, full of hope, full of opportunity.

'Same again?' the young barman asked.

Charlie nodded.

9

Charlie and Robbie had one more drink before parting company, much to Robbie's disappointment.

That said, they agreed he would pick Charlie up at 8am in Ashford tomorrow morning.

The men said their goodbyes and Charlie started walking back towards the Burstin to pick up his belongings and check out.

This was the end of a dark part of his life. He felt that old, familiar warmth return. Tara's warmth. Love returning.

The dilapidated exterior of the old hotel epitomised the wreck his life had become. He knew the direction he needed to go in. This would be the last time he would be back here.

Alcohol had become such a fundamental part of his broken life. As Charlie walked to the station, five minutes until the fast train to Ashford, he saw the welcome lights of the Co-operative supermarket beckoning him in. The bright colours of gin and vodka cans whispering like a siren.

Consume, young man. Consume.

The thought of more drinks for the train sent a warm buzz through his body. He stopped and let it go, let it pass and went in and grabbed an iced coffee.

On the train, Charlie felt a transformation. Shaking off the chrysalis, urging himself forward, yet back, back to his old life; comfort, contentment, stability.

He texted Tara, *On my way xxx*, as he watched the green fields of East Kent speed by.

His phone buzzed, a smiley face blowing a kiss.

Walking through the cycle lanes by the river from Ashford Central, all was quiet, the trees swayed in the breeze.

Charlie breathed. He stopped at the Tesco at the bottom of Hythe Road and picked up flowers and a bag of Salted Caramel M & M's for Tara.

The road was a long, slow uphill curve past the garage, over the train tracks, through to the Windmill pub. He looked into the gloom and saw Jake and Tracey, the owners, standing by the bar. He waved, they beckoned him in, he smiled but continued walking.

He stood outside of their cosy end of terrace and stared.

It was all he ever wanted. A beautiful wife whom he loved.

Comfort, contentment, security. Comfort, contentment and security.

It was to be his mantra, so he never forgot this feeling again. Never allowed it to leave.

He opened the wooden gate, closing it quietly. Made his way through the front garden, weeds overgrowing. Up to the patio door. He got out his key just as the door opened and there she stood.

'Welcome home,' she said, smiling.

Charlie fought back tears, taking off his shoes at the door, feeling the warm soft carpet beneath his toes.

Tara had redecorated the front room. The two rubber plants they bought when they moved in adorned two corners of the room. The leather Winchester sofas had been swapped around and the foot stool had been recovered in a burnt orange silk.

There was a clean, white rug covering the wooden floor and Tara's salt lamp created a homely, orange glow.

Charlie smiled and nodded at his fiancée, pleased with the improvements.

'Hungry?' she said, returning the smile.

Charlie hadn't thought about it, but since the butterflies had left his stomach they were replaced by a want for food.

He nodded again.

'OK, sit.' Tara said, going to the kitchen.

Charlie did as he was told and took a seat on the sofa.

He listened to the clunking of plates, the signs of domestic life that always seemed to allude him.

It was a far cry from endless kebabs and the noise of the TV which was his soundtrack at the Burstin.

After a few minutes, Tara returned with two plates of pasta: steaming hot and with scents of cream and garlic.

She returned to the kitchen and brought Charlie

a glass of white wine, Tara stuck to the lemonade.

'Glad to be back?' She asked. 'You like what I've done with the front room?'

'I missed it. It's beautiful.'

'Thanks. What's been going on?'

'That can wait. How are you? How's the…' Charlie nodded towards Tara's stomach, while wrapping spaghetti around his fork.

'The baby, Charlie? The baby is fine!' Tara chuckled, watching Charlie's polite nervousness tickled her.

'How are you feeling?'

'Well, tired all the time really. Lots of naps during the day, which is nice…' Tara smiled.

'Suits me…' Charlie smiled.

'If only you didn't have to work…' Tara said, with a coy smile.

'Yeah, about that.'

'Go on…'

'Well, I kind of quit.'

Tara looked surprised.

'Yeah, I know,' Charlie continued. 'I mean it sounds mad. But really, it is for the best you know. They pulled the Wood job.'

'What?'

'Yep.'

'After all that guy has done to you? To us?' Tara's voice rising an octave.

'I know. I know.'

'What the hell are they thinking?'

'It came from 'up top.' That's all I know.'

Tara harrumphed. 'So what? He's pulled some strings and got the Super to shut the case down?'

'Looks that way…'

'Goodness me. What are you going to do?' Tara asked, putting her plate on the floor next to the new white rug.

Charlie shot her a glance and she knew.

'I don't want you to do anything dangerous, Charlie... but I do think you need to do something about all of the death and the kids and stuff. Anything I can do to help…' Tara offered.

'Thanks, but I reckon this is a solo mission, this time. I have lost one daughter. I can't lose anyone else that I love.'

10

The phone was buzzing. Charlie couldn't believe he'd left his phone on vibrate.

'Turn it off…' Tara mumbled, half asleep.

Charlie looked at it, *Robbie*.

He put the phone on silent and pulled the cover back over his head.

Three loud parps from a car horn outside shattered the serenity. Charlie sighed and checked his phone again.

Robbie was still ringing.

'Hi, Robbie.'

'All right son? Good night was it?' The voice on the other end was upbeat, chipper.

'Err, yeah…. so uhm…' Charlie mumbled.

'Yeah, yeah, you're not ready, you're still in bed, whatever…'

'Uhm…'

'Right, I'm going to MacDonald's for brekko, you've got ten minutes. Wash your bollocks and meet me outside, all right? We got a prick to catch!'

'OK. Cheers, Robbie.'

The phone went dead and Charlie heard the sound of screeching tyres.

He got back into bed and snuggled into Tara.

'You got to go?' she said softly.

'Yeah. If we want to get Troy Wood…'

'You got to go then…' she said, closing her eyes and rolling over.

Charlie raised himself and headed for the shower. He was like heavy timber, creaking.

He opted for a cold, three-minute soldier's shower to wake him up. The sun blinked through the blinds.

He got out, brushed his teeth and looked at his face for the first time in a long while.

A layer of stubble had been his mask for the weeks he was in exile. He grabbed the razor and filled a bowl of warm water.

He looked deeply into his pale, green eyes. Sadness, pain, darkness. But there he was. Rebuilding.

He finished and wiped himself with a towel. Back in the bedroom, Tara had fallen back asleep.

He got changed into an open neck shirt and a pair of brown chinos, put a dab of wax in his hair and styled it to the right. A splash of Issey Miyake and Charlie felt ready for the day.

He kissed Tara on the forehead, who snuffled into her pillow, and then he went down the stairs and out the front of the house and waited.

He checked his phone. A habit he had gotten into a little too much recently.

There was nothing of any interest to him on social media.

He checked the news and noticed reports that cases of this mysterious virus were increasing rapidly in the country. Charlie took a deep breath, just as Robbie pulled up in his silver

BMW.

He jumped into the passenger seat while Robbie passed him a McMuffin.

'What did you get me?'

'Double Sausage and Egg, obviously!' Robbie said, with a mouthful of food.

Charlie nodded.

'Where to then, boss man?'

'The glorious sights and sounds of downtown Dartford,' Charlie said, unwrapping his muffin.

'Righto,' Robbie said, pulling away. 'You can fill me in on the way up there.'

'We need to start at Thraxin. Their main headquarters are up there. I have been doing a bit of digging around and I think there is some sort of connection between the Wolfire company owned by our boy Troy, and the big pharma companies.'

'Well, that wouldn't be a surprise would it? There's been dodgy dealings between powerful business and them for years…' Robbie smiled.

'You reckon?'

'Well, why is it you think people get sick every winter?' Robbie asked.

'Erm… cold weather?'

'Nah, mate. You can't get sick from the cold weather. *Fact.*' Robbie stated.

'Then why do people get sick and old people are more likely to die when the temperature drops?'

'These companies mate! Pumping out illnesses, different strains. That's what I reckon…' Robbie mused.

'Isn't that just a conspiracy theory?' Charlie added.

'Yeah, I mean it could be. But how comes people get different sicknesses and different illnesses? Surely your body would build up an immunity to the common cold and flu? Why is it always evolving and changing?'

'Dunno, Rob. You tell me.'

'To keep the drugs flying out! It makes sense. New viruses, new drugs, more money for big fuckin' pharmacuticle gaffs.'

'Pharma-what, mate?'

'Pharmasoo…pharmakutisal…pharma…   oh, fuck it! You know what I mean!' Robbie said, hitting the steering wheel with his hand.

'Pharmaceutical, dear…' Charlie said smiling and patronisingly patting his arm.

Robbie looked at Charlie.

'No one likes a smart cunt, Char.' They both laughed as Robbie put his foot down.

'Have you heard about this new virus then?' Charlie asked tentatively.

Robbie was ready to burst. 'This is what I mean! Some dirty virus, concocted in a lab somewhere. Just this time they didn't want it to get out. It was released too early. Now they are all blaming it on China!'

'Hm,' Charlie was unconvinced. He enjoyed Robbie's theories and debated whether to challenge him on them, but thought better of it.

Robbie looked over again.

'Come on, Charlie. You don't believe some geezer ate a bat and caused all this malarkey do you?'

'The world is a dark place mate, and I haven't got a clue anymore.'

Robbie decided to change the subject.

'So, what's the plan up there, Char? What are you looking for exactly?'

'Well as far as I can see we are going to have two options…'

'Right…'

'Well, we can go and ask for a meeting with the director of the company…a… Mr. Garrett…' Charlie said looking at the notes that he had made on his phone.

'When that doesn't work, what's our plan B?'

'I don't know… I thought maybe you could create a diversion and I could sneak in…' Charlie suggested, looking over at Robbie.

Robbie nodded in approval, but he looked like he had something else he wanted to say.

'What do you think?' Charlie asked.

'To be honest, I was just keen on going through the front door. You know, smashing our way in.' Charlie waited and looked at his pal in disbelief. Robbie looked back.

'Wh-What?' Robbie said, looking confused.

Charlie burst into laughter.

'It usually works for me!' Robbie retorted and both men laughed. 'Go on then, son, we'll try it your way and if it all goes tits up… my way!'

'Well let me try plan A, get a meeting. Then plan B, sneak in and see what I can find. Worse case and all goes wrong we can go to your plan, OK?' Charlie said.

'Yes, mate. Plan C. I got some balaclavas in the boot in case we need them!' Robbie said.

'Balaclavas?'

'Yeah, I love them. They proper keep your face nice and warm. Got a bad rep because of East End Gangsters, but I reckon they could make a comeback!'

Charlie chuckled. He couldn't take Robbie seriously but he really enjoyed his company. It was as if he had known him for years.

His phone vibrated in his trouser pocket. It was a number he didn't know.

'Hello?'

'Charlie, it's Darren Jackson.'

'Calling me from a different number now, Jacko?'

'Well, I knew you wouldn't answer!' he replied.

'Boss, it's not going to work…'

'Just hear me out, will you?' Jackson said, raising his voice. 'I know how it makes you feel, Charlie. If it's any consolation I was fuming when I heard the case had been pulled. You are no dummy though. You know what's going on here…'

'Yes. Friends in high places. Troy Wood's murky ascent to the top means he can basically have what he wants. Means he is not accountable, right?'

Charlie realised why Jackson was on a new phone number. He wouldn't want this call to be overheard.

'Obviously he is accountable. And you are right to be furious, but the system is the system, corrupt though it may be. They don't want to be seen going after him.'

'Despite what he's done? All the murders? The kids?'

'Despite what he's done.'

'And that's why I have to leave. You understand that, right?'

'I know you are angry. I know how much it means. So, I'm going to put you on leave until you want to talk about it.'

'I don't want to talk about it. I want justice to be served!'

Jackson sighed.

'It's just not black and white, Charlie.'

'It is to me.'

'Right, well, you're on leave. Don't do anything stupid.'

'Char, put the phone down. Who does he think he is?' Robbie chimed in, clearly catching the conversation. Charlie intimated for him to quiet down.

'I'm not coming back, Darren. That's it.'

'I'll speak to you soon.' Jackson muttered.

'Put the bloody phone down!' Robbie shouted.

Charlie ended the call.

'Calm down, Robbie! Technically he is still my boss, you know!' Charlie said, half serious, half buoyed by Robbie's bravado and devil may care attitude. It was rubbing off on him, for better or worse.

'Fuck him! If he doesn't respect what you've done on the 'right side of the law,' then let's see what happens when you do it on this side. With me.' Robbie muttered, a sinister edge to his voice.

'I want to try and keep it above board, if we can. OK? At some stage, once this is done, I am going to have to sort out my future.'

'Listen, Charlie, having me here in itself is an acceptance that you have taken a different path.'

Charlie nodded, he knew.

Dartford was a typically uninspiring, suburban town.

In the industrial commuter belt, rinsed by London of any character and joy. Like the paint in the pallet had mixed together, and the only colours that remained were grey and brown.

Charlie had attended school at the grammar here from 1992 until 1999 and to be honest, couldn't get out fast enough.

The final stab in the heart was the opening of Bluewater in the mid-nineties, a shopping centre in Greenhithe five miles to the east. It houses all the major department stores, retail outlets and eateries, and in one cut of a ribbon, made dirty

Dartford even less desirable.

Kebab shops, cheap colourful booze, pound stores, nail bars, Dartford became the blueprint for the twenty-first century British town.

Robbie drove sensibly along the one-way system and came to the large gates of the Thraxin building.

Fortunately, the gates were open, presumably for deliveries, but rather than drive in, the men parked up in a nearby side road.

Charlie pulled out a small lockpicking device and a taser from the pack he had placed in the boot of Robbie's car.

'What's that? You want something a bit more you know…. meaty?' Robbie said smirking.

Charlie gave Robbie a sideways glance which told him everything Charlie thought about that suggestion.

'I'll wait for you out here, old boy, while you unsuccessfully attempt plan A,' Robbie said, lighting a cigarette and leaning against the large, stone wall that flanked the building.

Charlie smiled.

'Right, wish me luck.'

'Yeah, text me if you need me.'

11

Robbie nodded as Charlie walked through the gates and towards the large, double doors into the building.

'Excuse me, sir… can I help you?' the guard in a booth shouted over to Charlie.

'Yes, sorry. I have an appointment,' Charlie said, not breaking stride, pointing at the double doors.

'I haven't got any appointments scheduled here?'

Charlie stopped and changed approach, walking towards the booth. The guard looked down at a diary, turning the pages.

'Sorry, yes. It was organised with Mr Garrett late last night. He knows I'm coming. My name is Allan Donald from the Wolfire Group. If you want me to wait here with you, while you check it out, that's fine. Or I can reschedule, but that won't be ideal,' Charlie said, looking directly at the guard.

'Let me just check,' the guard said, picking up a walkie talkie.

'Yeah… Hi Dan, are you there?' Charlie waited with trepidation. 'Tango, you reading?'

There was a crackle and fizz on the radio.

'Roger.'

'Yeah, I have got a…. Mr Donald from the… Wolfire Group here. Says he has an appointment with Mr Garrett.'

'Hm…. Nothing here, I'm afraid.' The voice said. 'Send him up anyway.'

'Sure. I'll get him to buzz in. OK, up to the double doors, press the buzzer.'

'Thanks,' Charlie said.

He was buzzed in and stood opposite a huge wooden desk in the reception area. A security guard stood behind it. There were some large green Bamboo plants that adorned the office space, which looked wildly out of place in this style of sterile building.

'Hi there,' Charlie said softly.

'Mr Donald? Let me see.' The security guard stared at him. 'That's strange. Mr Garrett is off-site today. What was it regarding?'

'Oh, it must be a mix up, I can reschedule if it's easier…' as Charlie spoke, he took a moment to survey the surroundings, the entrances in and out. There was a main door to the offices that were shut and an open door behind the reception area.

'It's very odd. He doesn't usually forget his appointments. Let me call him.' The security guard said, picking up the phone.

'Oh, it's OK. Don't worry, I'll speak with him and change it…'

The security guard was not going to be moved though. He waited on the end of the line. Charlie had to think fast.

'Actually, can I speak to him?' Charlie leaned over as if to grab the phone and stuck the security guard in the neck with the taser he had pulled from his pocket.

The guard convulsed; his wide eyes met Charlie's.

'Sorry, pal…' Charlie said, as he eased the guard to the floor, unconscious.

He texted Robbie, *moving to plan B*.

Charlie noticed that there were a number of security camera images on the computer screen behind the desk.

He felt the wires down the back of them which led to a large black box, where the footage would be held.

He disconnected the box and put it under his arm.

Charlie moved towards the main door and looked in through the glass. There were two members of staff at a table, working.

Charlie went to the other double door and pushed it which led him into an empty corridor.

He swung the door open and tiptoed down it. There were small laboratories on either side, some with staff working in them, others empty.

Charlie continued along and realised quickly he couldn't carry on walking through the building as he was.

He checked one of the rooms to his right, which was empty so he went in. In front of him stood a large, silver device that he knew was used to mix different ingredients.

There was no-one around and the machine was

silent. He spied a small office towards the back of the large room. There were a number of boiler suits in plastic bags, sitting on one of the metal shelving units. He unwrapped one and put it on, thinking it could only help him get through the building unquestioned.

Charlie left the room and carried on up the corridor. He passed a man in a lab coat who nodded at him. Charlie smiled.

He carried on walking up a small flight of stairs, into a large office space. The light streamed through the large glass windows across the open plan desks, making Charlie feel vulnerable.

That said, he felt he must be going in the right direction as he was off the factory floor and in a more civilised environment. He could feel the aircon cooling his face and there were green bamboo plants in the corners, and abstract paintings adorning the wall.

He waited in a corner of the open-plan office. There were at least eight workers he could see, staring at screens, removing papers from photocopiers, drinking coffee.

Charlie couldn't see a way to get to Garrett's office without getting noticed, so he got out his phone, texting Robbie, *I need plan C pretty urgently. Plan B is not going to work!*

Charlie crouched in the corridor, waiting for the two blue ticks to arrive.

'Hey? What are you doing up here?'

A man in a brown shirt and orange tie came

closer to Charlie, who nodded and apologised before scarpering back down the stairs and out of a fire exit door, which lead to an exterior stairway.

He checked his phone.

Roger, it said. Charlie waited a number of minutes, wondering what Plan C might look like with Robbie at the helm.

Suddenly, an almighty thunder crashed through the building, as if part of the roof was caving in.

The bang turned into a loud, metallic scraping sound.

'What the hell is that?' One of the men on the ground below shouted.

An alarm sounded and a bright red light started flashing in the corner of the room.

Charlie waited a few moments listening for sounds on the other side of the door to ensure the coast was clear before re-entering the building.

Creeping back through the corridor the red flashing lights provided backdrop... the sound of the alarm, deep and deafening.

Charlie went up the stairs and through the office space that was now empty.

At the end of the space there were further offices, Charlie had to work quickly, trying to decipher which one would be the jackpot. There was a small alcove to his right and another more ornate door within it.

Charlie went to it. It had a gold plate that read,

Director.

He quickly grabbed the lockpick from his pocket and began working the lock. Charlie enjoyed the adrenaline buzz, the fact that he was back at it, even without the protection of the badge. That did remind him, he needed to work quickly and leave no trace. Except of course the security guard, but perhaps that could be explained as the guy just passing out.

Eventually the lock gave way and Charlie turned the knob and opened the door.

Slipping inside, he surveyed the notice boards, and the desk in front of him. He slid the drawers open and found nothing of note.

There was a safe on the wall which he inspected. It was small, and secured tightly.

There was no way he could open it with the meagre implements he had brought with him, so he thought about getting it off the wall and taking it with him, which is a skill he had become quite accomplished at in recent years.

There was nothing in the room sharp enough to prise it away, so Charlie began elbowing the safe to see if it would budge.

He was anxious about the noise but also intrigued by the contents of the safe. He continued to hit it until his elbow went numb, hoping the ringing of the alarm masked the bangs.

'Hey! What are you doing in here?' Came a voice from the office door. Charlie looked up to see two police officers entering the room.

'Alright gents. This is my office; I just left the key at home...' Charlie said as confidently as he could.

The first copper who was taller than the other smirked and started moving closer.

Charlie moved further behind the desk.

'Course it is, Charlie!' the policeman laughed. 'You are going to be coming with us, pal.'

Charlie was confused. Perhaps the coppers had seen him on the TV? Maybe they were Folkestone nick and he didn't recognise them? He had been on what felt like permanent leave since the end of the Rosenkreutz case.

'Well, you know... I don't really fancy coming with you guys...' Charlie moved further to the back of the room, unsure of what he was going to do to get out of this tangle.

'Oi! Oi!' followed by a deep thud, as a long black crowbar thrust into the first policeman's diaphragm.

The guy nearer to Charlie looked aghast. He was panicked. Robbie moved beside Charlie, glowering.

'Alright, son?' Robbie said.

'Let him go, Rob. This fella doesn't want any trouble,' Charlie said, eyeing the copper.

'Nah, fuck him. This prick has been following us since Maidstone services, so he must know what he's got himself into...who he was dealing with…'

The copper laughed again, 'Oh yeah. You're such a tough guy! A tough guy with a crowbar...'

'God, I hate old bill, Char. You really are the exception…'

With that Robbie swung the bar and hit the copper square across the face. It knocked him unsteady.

'Robbie, leave him!' Charlie said, moving around from behind the desk.

It was too late however, as Robbie swapped hands and swiped at him again. Droplets of claret danced across the sterile office.

The policeman fell to the floor, unconscious.

'Jesus, Robbie!'

'Mate grow a pair, will ya?' Robbie shouted, staring at Charlie.

The two wolves stared each other down, in silent confrontation.

Charlie calmed and realised that he would probably be nicked if it wasn't for his partner in crime here. He had joined the dark side, in bed with the devil. Sure, Charlie could rationalise that it wasn't him who raised his hand to the two police officers, but he didn't stop Robbie. He allowed it, he was an accomplice.

Charlie did not want to get caught and ruin the slim chances left of a life with Tara and their unborn baby.

'Here pass me that, will you?' Charlie asked.

The alarm stopped, the red lights turned back to normal and Robbie threw the bar at Charlie.

Charlie grabbed it with both hands and then plunged down on the safe with full force.

'Here Charlie, I reckon you have about two minutes until all of these bods are back...'

Charlie kept banging the safe, which was loosening.

'Come on then muscles...' Charlie said, inviting Robbie over.

They swapped and within two smashes, the safe was off the wall and scooped up in Robbie's large paw.

'Clearly, I loosened that...' Charlie said.

'Oh yeah, clearly...' Robbie said, joining his partner at the door.

They could hear voices along the corridor.

'Fuck!' Robbie said, a little too loudly.

'Window?' Charlie suggested.

They nodded at one another and Robbie went back to the office as Charlie closed the door and locked it from inside.

Robbie used the safe to break the glass before clearing the rest of the shards with his elbow.

'Bit of a drop...' he said.

Charlie had a look. It was probably about ten feet.

'Yeah... no other option though, mate.'

'OK...' Robbie passed Charlie the safe and manoeuvred his large frame onto the ledge.

'Here goes...'

'Roll when you reach the ground, don't land on...'

'...Bruv, you think I'm an amateur?'

'No comment...' but before Charlie had finished the sentence Robbie had gone, rolled and was back on his feet.

There was someone behind Charlie rattling the doorknob and shouting.

'Here!' Charlie threw the safe and CCTV box down to him, before launching himself to the ground.

He landed awkwardly and twisted his knee a little. It was as if Robbie knew and grabbed him, bringing him back to his feet.

Charlie was struggling, so Robbie put his arm around his friend and used him as support out of the gates, past the police vehicle and a few stragglers from the building who eyed them suspiciously.

The men fled back to the car and jumped in, just in time to see in their rear-view mirror two police cars pulling into the grounds.

12

'Successful first job?' Robbie said, driving sensibly back towards Dartford's one-way system.

'Depends on how you look at it, Rob. I mean, risking our lives, assaulting coppers, theft from a private building… not great.'

'Yeah, but we weren't caught, were we? They can't pin any of that on us!'

'Hm. I suppose not. Anyway, let's see what's in this safe before we start slapping each other's backs. Cheers for having my back in there,' Charlie said, inspecting his leg.

'Any time. How's the leg? You fell badly...'

'Sore.'

'Nothing an ice pack and a bottle of vodka won't solve,' Robbie grunted and turned up the nineties dance tune that was playing on the radio.

'Rob, how did you get the alarm to sound?'

'Funny one really. When I got your text, I was milling around the warehouse out the back...'

'Trespassing...?'

'Well... scoping the area. There was an old JCB digger out there. The company are 'expanding their operations' I overheard...'

'Sounds about right...'

'So yeah, thought I still knew how to drive the thing from my days on site. Turns out I didn't.'

'So?'

'So, I kind of put the digger arm through the top floor of the building...'

Charlie looked at Robbie and they both laughed.

'That would have been the crunch I heard.'

'Yeah, so the thing got stuck in the roof and I couldn't pull it out. There were bricks and tiles falling down, but I couldn't dislodge it. I thought it best to lay low until I saw the old bill enter. I'd been watching and they had followed us in an unmarked car.'

'Really? I didn't see them,' Charlie said surprised.

Robbie grunted.

'I went back to the car for the crowbar and then scooted around to the side fire exit as the alarm was going off. Looks like I made it just in time.'

'Oh no, I had it covered, Robbie. I was just taking a subtler approach.'

'Righto,' Robbie sniggered. Charlie laughed and punched his mate on the shoulder.

'Cheers, pal.'

'Now, to get this safe open,' Robbie said. 'I know just the man.'

They drove back to Folkestone, listening to the loud music Robbie had put on and collecting their respective thoughts.

At junction thirteen of the motorway the car pulled off and Robbie drove carefully towards the Park Farm industrial estate. It was 2.30pm.

'Cheeky MaccyDs?'

'Well yeah. I think we've earned it.' Charlie

concurred.

Robbie pulled into the drive thru and the men ordered a burger meal each.

They sat in the car and polished off their food before Robbie continued along to Brockman Road in the centre of town.

He parked up, picking up the safe, and the two men got out.

Robbie checked the area to make sure he wasn't seen by anyone before jumping up the few steps to the door.

He pressed the buzzer before entering into the porch area and out of sight.

Charlie followed him.

The door buzzed and Robbie pushed it open to reveal a dilapidated hallway that was dark and bare.

He continued up a flight of stairs and came to another wooden door.

He knocked three times and there was a shuffle behind the door. It opened a crack.

'Who's this?' a gruff, male voice said.

'All right Trev, it's me.'

The door opened and the two men crept in.

Trevor looked Charlie up and down.

'Part of the establishment, eh? The system, the corporate conspiracy keeping us all disparate, angry and alone, eh?' Trev said as he shut the front door behind them. Charlie was concerned how Trevor knew he was a copper just by looking at him, but decided not to push the matter.

Charlie looked at Robbie who had plonked himself in one of two chairs in the small box room. Trev was heading towards the other behind a desk and had four large computer screens on it.

'Trying to bring it down actually,' Charlie said.

Trev nodded, sitting behind the desk.

'Got this safe, Trev. Couldn't open it for us carefully mate? We need whatever is inside.' Robbie asked.

'The police are just a facet of the system. Guardians of the elite, oppressing the vulnerable, while protecting their own,' Trev continued.

Charlie couldn't be bothered to argue in his current state of mind.

'Yeah, sure. About the safe?' Charlie asked.

'Hm, yeah. Give us a couple of hours.'

Robbie nodded at Trev and the men left his flat and went back down the stairs.

At the bottom Charlie texted Tara.

Everything OK? X x x

She read it quickly and responded.

Sure. What time you coming back? X x x

Couple of hours nearly done x x x

Okie dokie x x x x x

'Here Charlie, let's leave the motor here and go get a pint yeah?' Robbie suggested.
'Go on then.'
It was too early for Junction 13 to be open so they went to Harvey's Wine Bar.
Robbie ordered a pint of Stella and Charlie had a diet coke.
Robbie, as always, sat so that he was facing the door of the building.
He checked his phone and sighed.
'Whats up, bud?' Charlie asked.
'Becky...'
'I see...'
'The other night when we went out, I came back to hers, but she's still got the hump about Laura.'
'Did you go straight back?'
'Well... no, but I did go back. I just stayed out a bit longer first...'
'How much longer?'
'Couple of hours...'
Charlie couldn't help but smile.
'Well at least you went back.'
'Wish I hadn't bothered mate, the amount of grief I get.'
Robbie's phone rang and he went outside to take it.
Charlie got up after finishing his drink and went to find his friend.
He could hear Robbie's voice raised, angry on

the phone.

Charlie made eye contact.

Robbie looked at him and mouthed the words Junction 13.

The men started walking. Robbie stayed on the phone, talking quietly once again in monosyllables.

Charlie's knee was twisted for sure and he was hobbling along Sandgate Road in some pain. He was getting older and with every move he felt the urge to call a taxi and spend the rest of the evening on the sofa with Tara.

He wanted the contents of the safe though, so struggled on towards the next destination.

Robbie eventually got off the phone and was talking like he was ready for a night out.

Charlie firmly rejected this idea, much to his friend's chagrin.

'See how you go, Charlie. Have a cheeky beer up the Junction and then go from there, eh?' Robbie said, a hint of desperation in his voice.

'Not tonight, Robbie. I need the contents of that safe, then I'm off. I don't feel great.'

'We can get Sharn to put an ice pack on your leg, eh?' he continued, not prepared to be placated.

'No, I need to get home really and rest it properly,' Charlie asserted.

Robbie said nothing, as they rounded the corner past the florists and toward the door of the small bar.

Through the glass doors, Charlie could see Trev

sitting in a corner booth, with a short drink, looking shifty.

Charlie went in, nodded at Trev and sat opposite him.

Robbie followed.

Charlie saw a manila envelope on the table which he tapped with his right finger.

'Your documents, sir,' he said with mock sincerity.

'Thanks. Let me pay you something...' Charlie started.

'Err... that will not be necessary, thank you.' Trev said.

'At least let me buy you a drink...'

'Once again, I will have to pass. This place is too... open plan for someone like myself to be. My work is done here.'

Trev nodded at Charlie before shuffling to the exit, leaving the envelope in front of them on the table.

'I'll get drinks,' Robbie said.

'I'm all right,' Charlie said.

'Come on, Charlie, just one?'

It was more of a demand than a request, so Charlie caved and agreed. It was a part of Robbie's personality he was not overly keen on. Overbearing and dominating... but Charlie convinced himself it came from a good place, and that Robbie's positive attributes outweighed the negative.

Charlie snuck a peek into the envelope and

noticed letters and a small black Dictaphone.

Robbie returned to the table.

'Hit jackpot, have we?' he asked.

'Difficult to say. There could be some audio of interest, or why would it be in a safe?'

Robbie nodded.

'Stick it on then,' he said.

'No. Not here.' Charlie said, a little surprised by Robbie's devil may care approach.

Robbie tutted and looked out of the window.

'Listen, Robbie cheers for today. I really mean it.'

'It's all good. I told you I would help you get this guy and that's what I'll do.' Robbie was short, probably a little disgruntled he had lost his wingman for the night. For all of his loyalty, he had dangerously needy traits also.

Charlie finished his drink and Robbie watched him as he began to assemble his belongings, ready to leave.

'Until tomorrow then,' Robbie exhaled.

'Yes, what are you up to later?'

'Unsure yet. May meet some fellas down Sandgate. May head down the Harbour.'

'Well, see you tomorrow buddy,' Charlie said heading out the door.

Robbie ordered another drink and picked up his phone.

He dialled and waited.

'Hello?' a stern, female voice answered.

'Listen, Becks… let's try and sort this out, eh?'

There was a pause.

Robbie waited. He was tired and had just enough drink in him to want to make amends and settle in for the night.

'Babe, you need to sort this out though, y'know? Are you drunk?'

'Nah of course not! I've just had a couple...'

'Hm. Well, go on then...'

'Look, I just don't want to argue. I can't help the way I am. You know what you signed up for when you got with me. You know what I'm like.'

Robbie rattled it off, like a script. He had said it many times before, it was just the recipient who changed.

'I didn't sign up for this. You said you wanted to get out of it all. Away from the life. Settle down, somewhere away from all the pricks in Folkestone...'

'And I do. Listen, just let me come over and we can talk, yeah?'

Pause.

'I'll bring you meat and chips...?'

'Go on then, fifteen minutes. Order the food now and come straight, all right?'

'All right, babe.'

Robbie put the phone down and felt an unfamiliar warmth.

He rang the food through straight away, and ordered a whisky chaser from Sharn.

Robbie downed it, said his goodbyes and walked around to the taxi rank outside Sainsburys.

'Densole, mate. But just need to stop at the Kebab house around the corner,' Robbie said, getting into a taxi.

'Sure thing, boss.'

13

Robbie picked up the food and scaled Hawkinge Hill towards Becky's place. He felt excited to be seeing her, but also trepidation. He never knew how things would go between them.

He paid the driver and carried the plastic bag of fast food to her door.

He knocked and waited. She took longer than he wanted her too to answer.

Eventually the door slowly opened, Becky stood in just a towel, her hair wet and hanging in blonde ringlets above her soft, tanned skin, courtesy of the Sun Shop on Sandgate Road.

'Alright,' he said and walked in placing the food on the side.

He put his arms around her and undid the towel which dropped to the floor.

Picking her up, he placed her gently on the kitchen worktop. Her grey eyes bore into him. They longed for him, but a version of him he promised to be, but never was.

'Babe...' she said, feigning unwillingness, but she couldn't convince herself, let alone her partner.

She pulled him to her and kissed him hard.

Her nakedness and vulnerability melted into desire and lust, feeling for his belt buckle and fly, buoyed by the hardness beyond the zip.

He pulled away from her kiss briefly and smiled, before taking her tongue into his mouth again.

Becky released him from his jeans and gently

slid him inside her.

She moaned at his girth and pulled him closer to her. The scent of cigarettes and alcohol, a strong aphrodisiac, as he thrust into her golden body.

She wrapped her legs around him, gripping his back, talons digging into his dark gilet.

The climax rose in her slowly, the vibrations of his deep thrusts, the colour and the chaos... Her vision blurred as he thrust his last inside her and she held him into her, tighter.

Robbie allowed her to hold the embrace for a moment, before pulling himself away.

She shuddered as they moved apart. He went to his pocket and grabbed his cigarettes as he opened the back door.

****

On the train back to Ashford, Charlie pulled out the documents from the safe.

The Wolfire logo appeared on the top of the headed paper.

He checked that there was no one sitting near him and began to read:

Dear Mr. Garrett,

I am pleased to confirm that my client is happy to go ahead with the agreement. If you would send the contracts to TW@wolfire.co.uk so we can proceed.

On behalf of my client and I, I wish to thank you for your co-operation in this matter.
Kindest Regards,

Robbie Helvig
Legal Secretary

Charlie flicked to the next letter:

Dear Mr. Garrett,

Documents received. Thank you for your prompt reply in this matter.

Kindest Regards,

Robbie Helvig
Legal Secretary

Charlie looked up the Wolfire company again on his phone. It was a media and PR company, based in Hoxton, London. So why were they doing deals with a large pharmaceutical company?

Charlie checked their information on the Companies House website and noticed that Troy Wood was listed as one of the trustees of Thraxin, in addition to being CEO for Wolfire.

He continued leafing through the documents in the manila envelope.

There were emails and letters all alluding to this

'deal'.

Charlie skim read the documentation, before landing on an email of note:

To: shelvig@wolfire.co.uk
From: ag@thraxin.com
Re:

Robbie,

We are having difficulties in our distribution network to the point where we don't see how it is going to be possible to meet the demands of your client, in the time frame that he insists upon.
Our head office is working overtime as it is and the schedule is just unachievable in its current format.
We need to readdress this at your earliest convenience.

AG

Charlie's interest was piqued:

To: ag@thraxin.com
From: shelvig@wolfire.co.uk
Re: Your message

Message from client: That won't do. My client is extremely unhappy. Please resolve ASAP.

Then there were no more documents, only the

dictaphone.

Charlie thought it best to listen to that at home, as the train pulled in to Ashford International Station.

14

'Hello, darling!' Tara said. She sounded genuinely pleased to see Charlie as he came through the door.

He was tired and took a shower to wake himself up for the evening.

'I made chicken salad,' Tara said as Charlie came downstairs in joggers and a hoodie.

'Awesome,' he said tucking in to a bowl thrust in front of him.

'How was your day?' she asked.

'Oh, eventful. Got some more leads. Think I may have a name for an associate in London, close to Wood.'

'Excellent, wanna show me?' Tara said, perching herself next to Charlie.

He was anxious about getting her too involved, but thought another pair of eyes and ears may help. He even enjoyed how they worked together in Hamburg. When they were... closer.

He lay the documents in front of her and she began to leaf through them.

'I wonder what this deal was, sounds serious?' Tara mused.

'And why are these two companies working together?' Charlie added.

Tara shook her head.

'What's on the tape?' she said, pointing to the dictaphone.

'Don't know yet,' Charlie said, reaching for it.

Tara suddenly reached over and kissed Charlie, touching his chest.

'I don't know what it is about this pregnancy, but it makes me feel a bit...' Tara didn't finish her sentence. Charlie flashed her a glance. She had a coy smile.

'Come on mister, let's go up to the bedroom...' she continued.

'Well, it would be rude of me to argue!' Charlie got up from the table and followed up the stairs.

Compared to when they first met, there was a bit more admin that went into their romantic time together. The rough and tumble, biting and clawing, replaced with teeth brushing and careful removal of garments.

Still, Charlie was not going to complain, he thought his life with Tara was over.

He thought he had destroyed it, like he had with Jo. If he could just get Troy Wood, then maybe, just maybe he could keep his life together. He knew that something in the documents he had would provide a clue.

'Erm, Charlie...? Back in the room, please...' Tara whispered, as she moved towards him.

'Sorry...' he said sheepishly.

There was a loud knock on the front door which brought the lovers from their desirous haze.

Tara took a sharp intake of breath and looked anxiously at Charlie.

He moved her aside, wrapping a towel from the bathroom around his waist and went downstairs.

Who could it be at this time of night? They both thought, but didn't say.

Charlie could hear Tara rushing to put clothes on as she came halfway down the stairs. Through the stained glass at the top of the old wooden door he could see a mop of hair.

'T, head back up, please,' Charlie said, concerned about her.

'Who is it?'

Charlie shrugged, and pointed back upstairs as Tara reticently retreated.

He looked at the latch and wondered whether he should put it on.

No, he thought to himself. *If someone has finally come for me, so be it.*

He opened the door fully, revealing a short man in shirt and trousers with a round, pink face.

The man looked relieved to see him.

'Mr Charlie Stone?'

Charlie felt the cold on his chest as he stood in front of the man, half-naked.

He heard Tara tiptoe half way down the stairs again.

'Yes?' Charlie said boldly.

The man looked up at Tara and read the situation.

'Sorry, mate. These are court papers. Hastings Family Court. You have been served, unfortunately.'

The man thrust the papers into Charlie's hands.

'Wait, what… who by?'

'All the information is in there. I'm sorry,' the man said, as he turned away shutting the porch door and then up the path.

15

'The bloody, horrible cow!' Tara said, not one prone to swearing or anger, but the added hormones may have well been playing a part.

'This is a new low,' Charlie said, deflated and beaten on the sofa.

'I just can't believe the absolute front of this witch! First, she stops you seeing Maddie without permission. Now she wants to change the bloody court order because she has moved further away!'

'She wants us to pay her legal bills too…'

'Are you actually kidding me?'

'Nope. It says so here…'

'How much?'

'Don't know, they are going to calculate it and email me later in the week,' Charlie was in shock.

'I can't bloody believe this. Well, we are going to go to this court date and win it. I'm serious Charlie. We are going to sit and write everything down and make sure they hear our version and get you your rights back…'

Charlie drifted off.

Would this world of hate and anger and sadness ever disappear? How could someone that only a few years ago professed to love him, want to take away all that he had? What drove people to those depths?

'… What date is it? OK… we have nine days. Plenty of time to get some legal advice and make sure we have a full, robust case…'

Charlie couldn't compute. He was numb from the pain and steely-eyed, and zombie-like he walked past Tara back upstairs and got changed. Tara followed him.

'What are you doing?' she asked.

'I love you. We can sort this tomorrow. I just need to get out for a bit.'

He kissed her.

'I love you, Charlie. Don't do anything stupid.' Tara shouted after him as he headed for the door.

16

The black abyss. The dark beyond the horizon. Charlie stared at the sea and wanted to find out what was there.

Was there darkness, blackness and nothing more?

The car drove itself to Dungeness. Charlie maniacally staring through the windscreen, aiming.

The desolation of the desert soothed him. The perfect metaphor for his soul.

He looked at the lighthouse. Its light did not shine, despite the night falling on East Kent.

He looked at the power station, smothering the skyline: chugging, pumping, spewing.

The push and pull of the ocean called to him. Asking him to come forth, be at one with nature again, to be swept up in the comforting arms of the swell.

He moved closer in complete trance, stepping towards the ocean's edge.

He felt the cold, he welcomed it. He desired the numbness, he wanted not to feel anymore.

The water licked his brogues as his eyes remained open, glazed, empty.

'Oi, numbnuts? What the hell are you doing?' came a voice that rocked Charlie back to normality.

He turned to see Big Robbie's frame coming towards him, hands in pockets, bowling from side to side.

'What the hell are you doing here?' Charlie asked.

'You contacted me pal!'

'Oh, right… of course…' Charlie had no recollection of this.

'You… you erm, had some bad news eh, Charlie?'

'Oh, yeah. You could say that. It never rains, Robbie…'

'It pours…' Robbie finished off the sentence, looking at the ground.

Charlie walked back to his pal and welcomed his large bear hug.

'Come on then fella. Let's get you away from here, eh?'

Charlie followed Robbie in the car. He immediately felt lifted by his presence. He could hear the loud throb of music blaring as he drove at around 55mph along the 30mph roads of Romney Marsh.

Charlie couldn't help but smile at his outlandish behaviour.

They stopped at the bottom of Sandgate Hill and went into the Royal Norfolk Hotel.

'I don't usually come here,' Charlie said as the two men went to the bar.

'Exactly,' Robbie said, glaring at his friend.

Charlie knew what he meant. It was refreshing to be out of Folkestone, where nobody knew his name.

They sat down at a table with their drinks.

'Thanks for meeting me,' Charlie said. 'I feel a bit better already.'

'I thought you were heading out for a swim, when I found you. If you go out in that, you won't come back Char. Be careful!'

'I know, I know. It's just the sea, it… I don't know…'

'I do know. You want to swim out and not come back sometimes. I get it. I've been there.' Robbie said, looking the other way, frightening himself with the omission.

Charlie didn't look up, but he nodded.

'What's happened then?' Robbie said, pulling away and picking up his drink.

Charlie exhaled.

'It's the kid. I miss her. Really miss her, but Jo, she wants to stop me seeing her…'

'You what?'

'I've been 'summoned' to court. She thinks I'm a danger to Maddie…' Charlie's whisper was barely audible. He was on the verge of tears.

'I had this problem with a girlfriend once.'

'Wait, you have a child?'

'Yep… not allowed to see her now, obviously. She's um twelve now… or ten… I'm not sure…'

'What happened?' Charlie said interjecting. 'Why can't you see her?'

'Well, the ex-girlfriend didn't want me to see her. Same sort of bollocks as you. Bad influence and all that. So, I knew where they were drinking out in Fulham, back when I was in London...'

'Right...'

'Waited for her new boyfriend who was getting all chopsy down the phone and fucking smashed him sidewise with a golf club. Fella couldn't walk after. Had to have two pins in his leg. After that, they said I couldn't see her until she's older.'

'I see...'

'Well, I got him when he went out for a fag, it wasn't like she saw me do it, you know?'

'Yes, mate.' Charlie swallowed, wondering what, if any, lesson he could take from Robbie's tale.

'Give me the address, pal. I'll help you out here,' Robbie continued.

Charlie looked up at his big, simple friend. He put his hand on his shoulder.

'It's OK, Rob. I think we are going to have to do this the right way, I'm afraid.'

17

Charlie walked out into the cold night air.

Feeling better, a renewed sense of vigour ran through him.

He appreciated Robbie's understanding. Yes, he might take a different approach to him when it came to solving problems, but he was there for him when it mattered.

Charlie had to fight for his daughter, the same way he would have to fight to bring down Troy Wood.

He left Robbie once again in the pub. He had got the taste and wanted to continue drinking.

Charlie wanted to get a large bag of chips before going back home.

He went to the zebra crossing and then to the chip shop across the road.

The roads were quiet, as it was past ten o'clock, yet Charlie heard a car behind him: quiet, purring, cunning.

He turned to see a black Mercedes with tinted windows, heading through Sandgate towards Hythe.

Charlie took a second glance and stopped in his tracks.

He froze.

The black Mercedes: Green, Wadham, the cult. It was one of theirs.

The same low rider, top of the range, personalized number plates and tinted windows.

Charlie waited until it was past him, before sprinting back around the Royal Norfolk Hotel towards the car park and into his car.

It didn't take long until he was behind the Mercedes at a safe distance.

His heart was pounding. Panicking. All this should have ended. Who was in that car?

The Mercedes took a slow right turn up Hospital Hill, towards Temeraire Heights. Charlie watched from a distance as the car pulled into the private road that led into a drive.

Charlie pulled the car to a halt and proceeded on foot to the Corniche, which was the next road up.

The twinge in Charlie's knee had evolved into a thick grind, like two bones grating together. He tried to prevent it affecting his movement, gritting his teeth through the pain.

He wanted to get a view of Temeraire Heights below him, so he slid along the side of a house called Sandcastle and into the garden. He climbed the fence at the rear and found himself in a thinly wooded area.

The black Mercedes was below, between two large mansions that overlooked the English Channel. The car was parked, empty, but both buildings had lights on inside.

Charlie crept forward, trying to prevent putting too much weight on his right knee, as he moved through the darkness.

The small bushes that lined the affluent properties kept his cover as he moved between the two houses.

He listened for voices but heard nothing.

He made his way towards the first house, creeping into the garden and up to the back door. The doors and windows were closed but Charlie managed to sneak a look through the long curtains, covering the patio doors.

He saw a small girl, possibly three years old, running around and smiling. Peppa Pig was blaring from the TV and toys littered the cream rug in the living room.

He moved towards the second house, which was surrounded by a large wooden fence.

He had two options: go to the front of the house and around the side into the back garden, or over the fence.

Charlie felt that over the fence may be too risky, but he could gauge through the fence how safe it was to sneak in. There was a hole in one of the panels. The garden was dark, but there was movement in the house.

Two men were behind the glass of the back doors.

They were engrossed in some document, neither man looked up from it, so Charlie knew now was his moment to get nearer and infiltrate the property.

Charlie went over the fence as slyly as he could. Upon landing his footing slipped and he landed heavily on his right leg and drew a sharp intake of breath.

He waited a moment in pain, engulfed within it, until it slowly crystallised and turned to numbness.

The men were no longer poring over a document on the dining room table. They were not there.

Charlie sat like a predator, waiting for the next move.

He moved forward slowly behind a small brick wall that separated the patio from the grass.

Silence.

Charlie waited at the wall, breathing as quietly as he could.

He had been in this situation enough times and had to be very careful. It was possible his fall from the fence hadn't alarmed the men in the building. Yet experience taught him that men such as this, who live on their nerves and their instincts, had been alerted.

So, he stayed in the dark behind the wall, like a chess player waiting for a counter-move.

He slowly raised his head above the wall and in one movement the hunter had become the prey.

'Gotcha!' a voice whispered in his ear. He could feel the breath on his neck followed by an almighty crack on his temple.

18

Robbie watched his friend leave the Royal Norfolk Hotel, back to his happy home life.

He knew that he went out a lot, but all he wanted was for his mate to stay with him until closing time. Was that too much to ask?

Robbie pulled his phone from his pocket and went on to his incognito tabs.

He typed in adultjobs.co.uk and waited for the page to load. He checked that no-one was behind him, they never were, he was always careful to never leave his back to a door. Not in his line of work.

The page loaded and Robbie typed in the area as Folkestone, Kent. Available today. The page re-loaded.

Five options.

Robbie scrolled seeing what took his fancy.

Mayya was 23 years old, hot European body...

Danni was a 38-year-old MILF from Latvia...

Tori was a Busty British babe... *yeah, right*....

Robbie thought, of course she was.

These girls were always foreign, Eastern European, no concept of the lingo. Made getting the job done easier though, no awkward small talk.

Robbie put his phone back and mulled over his options. He went to the bar, ordered another pint of Stella and went out to have a cigarette.

The phone weighed heavy in his pocket. Guilt at

what he had done. How he had left it with 'her indoors'.

He opened the phone again and scrolled to Becky's number. He took a deep breath and rang it.

He waited, hoping it would be answered. Not so he could apologise, definitely not! Just so he could have the interaction.

No such luck, answerphone.

'Alright? Give us a ring. Let's talk, yeah?'

Robbie put the phone down and noticed the first three knuckles on his right hand, scabby and red.

He flicked his fag and went back in, leaning on the bar.

He opened the phone again and checked out his secret tab. *Mayya*...he decided.

He copied the number and sent the text.

R u avalible?

He sat the phone down on the side and surveyed the room, looking for something, someone, to change his mood.

****

There she was, Isla Fisher, Shannon, in her Summer Bay school uniform.

Charlie may have only been 8 years old, but he knew that Shannon was the type of girl he wanted to be hanging around with at school.

Her long, red hair and blue check uniform hung perfectly from her. Charlie felt butterflies that he hadn't before, and urged himself from the TV screen as the adverts kicked in.

Mum must have been in the kitchen... the light was on but nobody there.

Perhaps upstairs?

Someone must have been, his dad brought him home...

Charlie ran up the stairs, creaky, as always.

He checked all of the rooms, but no one was home.

Charlie felt panic rise through his body.

He checked the garden. Maybe dad was mowing the lawn.

Nope.

Charlie checked the front driveway. No cars present. That meant mum and dad were not here. Where was his sister?

The phone rings.

Maybe that was one of them.

Charlie gallops to the phone down the stairs, he nearly runs past it.

He picks up, phone goes dead. Charlie places the receiver down.

The phone rings.

Charlie picks up.

Breathing. Phone goes dead.

Charlie goes to the front room.

The phone rings.

Silence.

The phone rings.

WHO IS IT?

Dead.

The phone rings.

This continues for a few minutes. Charlie cries and cries uncontrollably. His eight-year-old mind cannot fathom this horrible adult world he has been thrust into.

The phone rings.

Mum comes home.

Charlie screams and weeps in her arms.

She cries too. She shouts.

Where is your father?

Yes, where is he indeed.

Charlie came too.

The cold ground was the first thing he felt, as his eyes opened slowly.... blurry...

He was in transit, somewhere cold and dark.

He moved to sit up, but his hands were tied. He stumbled and noticed blood across his clothes.

His right arm felt bruised and his mouth was tender.

His head pulsed as he managed to manoeuvre himself so he was leaning against the wall.

There was a metallic taste in his mouth. He spat. Red, yellows, greens.

'Oh, look who's woken up?' the same deep voice from the garden.

There was another crack to Charlie's skull and he was jolted out of consciousness once more.

Dad?

Yes, Mad… what's up?
Dad? Why can't you hear me?
I can hear you.
Dad? He can't hear me, I told you.
I hear you, sweetheart. I can hear you.
I'm giving up, there's no point. He can't hear me.
Maddie!

****

'There's a burger van about ten minutes down the road if you really hate it,' Arnold said.

'What on the industrial estate?'

'Yeah, just off from it, in the layby.'

'Hm.' Frankie pushed the lump of chicken around his plate.

'The way I see it, we are lucky to even get fed in here,' Arnold said.

'I don't mind paying for it, it's just the quality…' Frank said in a whisper, he didn't want any of the gargoyles behind the food-service counter to hear him. He shunted his plastic tray along, with his meaty hand. He was a thick set man, around five foot, eight inches. Square set, square head with sandy blonde hair. The tan he had picked up from his holiday in Turkey last year still glowed softly on his skin.

'I mean the place looks a bit brighter…' Arnold said optimistically. Arnold was thirty years older, with scruffy dark grey hair. His face was harder, sharper, with deeper lines. Arnold was taller, around six feet tall, yet scruffier than his younger colleague.

Frank looked around. It was dismal. A lick of paint and a few more plastic chairs. Oh, and the radio plays during lunchtime now. Hardly the Ritz, Frank thought to himself.

'I know what you're thinking, Frankie.'

'Oh yeah?'

'It's just not worth it. The current climate, all of this virus malarkey, country in recession. It isn't the right time to jump ship.'

'Hm.' Frank was thinking that his life could and should be better than this. Back in the good old days, it was tarts in mini-dresses and taking pills and coke off likely lads in the bogs.

Now here he was dealing with…. vermin.

'I mean, the pay is bloody good, Frank…'

'I know, but…it's the nature of-'

'-drop it out, mate. You knew what you were getting into. What, would you rather be back working the clubs all night?'

Frank smirked to himself. He was tired of the sermonising.

'Here, Arnie. If this is a processing facility for immigrants, then what's with that copper being held in number three?' Frank knew that the question would wind his boss up, but he didn't care.

'Well, it's not just a processing factory-'

'-Oh yeah, we are creating the vaccine too, I know you told me. Still, that fella? What's the ku?'

Arnold looked around, checking there were no other workers near him. He leaned in.

'I told you about him.'

'Did you? I don't remember.' Frank said nonchalantly.

Arnie took a deep breath.

'Yes. I did. He's what they call a dissident. He doesn't like the work we are doing here. So, he needs to you know... be kept in check.'

'So, that's why he's been black bagged and is barely breathing?'

'Listen, they found him in the bosses garden. Silly prick is off his nut, he could barely walk, trying to get in and kill him in his house!'

'Hm. Yeah, I guess. What's his problem with the boss anyway?'

'Fuck knows, Frank! Who cares? He is a problem. Trying to stop the company from doing business. If he does that, we don't get paid, and all this becoming public is not in our best interests.' Arnold stated.

Frank paused, swallowing a mouthful of dry chicken, washing it down with a gulp of warm orange squash.

'So why hasn't he been... you know...'

'Now that is a good question. You have a lovely brain, Frankie. Here's the thing, can you turn the bloody thing off when you are at work, yeah? I don't know why he's still alive, I don't know why the boss likes figgy pudding so much nor do I know what is behind the black door-'

'-All right, all right-'

'But what I do know is, the boss has asked us to keep him alive, and make sure he stays alive, by hook or by crook. That means when Carver gets a bit over-excited, you need to reign him in.'

'Understood, boss.'

'It's about time you went and checked on our guest anyway.' Arnold said.

He had no idea what went on in Frank's head. He didn't know why he couldn't just keep his head down, shut up and collect his pay packet.

'Of course, boss.' Frankie smiled, got to his feet and headed out of the canteen.

The usual suspects were out in the yard. Frankie had never been to prison, but he suspected the way the groups divided was very similar.

The Afghans in the corner. Always staring, always silent, menacing. Frankie had learned to ignore them.

Then there were the Syrian women who always stuck together, chatting to one another.

Then there were the boys. What looked like Romanian boys: shaved heads, skin and bone, playing football.

They made him shudder. What had these boys done to deserve being locked up in here?

Then there was the black door in the corner. The big, black metal one. With the whimpers and moans that came from behind it.

Frankie hated that door, so he quickened his

pace, getting out his security card to make it into the A block and towards 'the copper.'

He heard him before he saw him through the locked door. Inaudible moans, interspersed with cries of 'Maddie.' Frank wondered who she was. Sadness filled him. It didn't matter who it was. This... dissenter... was in absolute turmoil.

Frank slid the metal grate to one side and peered in. The copper's green eyes hit him first, piercing, staring up, not in desperation, but in rage.

The next thing was the stench. The copper had clearly had an accident or two and his makeshift toilet probably needed swapping out, but Frank was damned if he was going to do that.

'All right?' Frank asked, trying to sound cocksure, as if the whole situation didn't bother him.

The glassy green eyes never left him. The copper was scoping him out. Frank checked his firearm was there reassuringly attached to his left leg.

He checked that both ways were clear along the 'A' corridor, then went into his pocket and threw a few pieces of the left-over chicken into the cell.

'It's not a lot...'

The copper remained unmoved.

'For fuck's sake, Frankie. Quit it with that shit!' Arnold shouted, coming in and closing the door behind him.

'What?' Frank asked.

'You're going bloody soft!'

Arnold shifted him to one side and opened the door, squashing the pieces of chicken into the cold, stone floor.

'Here, grab that potty while you're in here!' Arnold called.

Frank sighed, stepped in and grabbed the metal tub.

The copper was sizing them up.

Arnold swung his leg at the copper's jaw, catching him a good one.

'Don't get any ideas, son!' Arnold shouted, as they both scarpered out and locked the door behind them.

The copper fell into a crumpled heap on the floor.

****

Robbie pulled up outside the old, Edwardian building on the west side of Folkestone.

The road had some misplaced, optimistic name... something Gardens.

He smiled to himself, thinking about all of the people who lived down here who had no idea there was a knock-in shop on their road, in their building, on the floor below them.

He got out of the car and put up his hoodie, lighting another cigarette, thinking about the wannabe hipsters, the arty trendy-types, the old money middle-aged Blue Harbour-wearing knobheads, who all thought they were special as they lived in The West End.

He went up to the door and knocked quietly, like the text said.

No. 43.

He waited.

There was shuffling behind the door. It opened a crack and then a little wider. Behind it, was complete darkness. He slid himself in and noticed an open bedroom door with a small side light.

He headed towards it, followed by little footsteps.

He turned to see 'Mayya,' behind him, smiling up at him, taking in his full frame, his strength, his size.

It was a bit of a lottery this part of the process, but Robbie was not appalled by what he saw.

She was older than her pictures suggested, but petite and shapely, probably a comfortable size twelve.

Mayya shut the door behind him.

'How long you like?' Mayya said softly.

'Half an hour,' Robbie grunted, already taking his shoes off. Mayya smelt the beer on his breath.

'OK, 70 please,' she asked.

Robbie ruefully went to his wallet and withdrew a wad of cash. He reticently pulled out the amount, preparing the notes slowly and carefully. If it was up to him, he would pay afterwards, but he knew that would be a no-go.

Not that he was worried. He just didn't fancy an unnecessary ruck with a gang of Eastern Europeans with baseball bats and shooters.

He handed over the notes and Mayya left the room with the money.

Robbie continued disrobing, down to his boxer shorts and then lay down on the bed.

Mayya returned, removed her slippers and began to take off her bra and knickers slowly.

'Nah. Come here.'

Mayya looked towards Robbie, with her big, brown eyes.

She did as asked, slowly, as Robbie reached out and yanked her towards him, grabbing her face and kissing her.

19

Charlie felt the sharp pain in the jaw and took a moment to collect himself.

He could hear the voices of the two men, arguing outside. He knew that one of them, the smaller, younger one, could hold the key to his escape.

The problem was, he didn't know where he was.

He remembered coming to in a truck on his way here. He was surprised that it was a vehicle that large, he was used to kidnappings in mini-vans or Transits, but he was sure from its low engine rumble that this was something bigger.

He looked around the cell. There was a roll-up mattress, a fresh metal bucket in the corner. No windows.

There was a small crack under the door that led outside, but that was it.

Charlie got to his feet. The pain in his knee hit him like a train and he crumpled again.

He could hear the voices of the men clearer now.

'Look, he can hardly stand,' Frankie said.

'Fuck him…' the voices trailed off. Charlie was used to hearing this type of old man in all walks of life; the same indoctrinated, authoritarian viewpoint. He could have been a copper, a politician or security for a shady criminal, it made no difference, the diatribe was still the same. He would get the job done, and do his master's bidding, regardless of the cost.

Charlie focused again on the younger man.

'...It doesn't mean we have to be...' his voice faded away as the men went out of the block and through another security door.

Charlie sat down on the mattress and thought of Maddie.

He needed to get out of here.

****

'I just don't get why you have to be such a prick about it!' Frank was beginning to get irate.

'I just don't get why you are in this job, Frankie! It didn't seem to matter to you when you were giving black eyes to kids with a bit of powder on them. But give this fucking lowlife a slap and you're whinging your bloody head off!' Arnold shouted.

'It's different!'

'Is it?'

Frank paused. 'Just lay off him a bit will you. He's fucked as it is. Crying out for some girl... he's broken. Whatever he's done to Wadham, he doesn't deserve all of this.'

Arnold was quiet as they went past the black door.

They could hear silence from behind it. An eerie, unpleasant silence.

'Here, Arn. You got clearance for that?' Frank nodded at the black door.

'You must be joking…' Arnold said, getting out his key and trying it anyway. The card reader came up red and he shrugged his shoulders.

As they turned and went away, through the black door came a low murmur that turned into a whimper.

Both men heard it, but said nothing. They continued to walk around the yard, as far away from the door as they could.

'Right, I'm off shift tonight. What are you doing?' Arnold asked.

'I'm on until midnight.' Frank replied.

'Well, here's an idea. Don't be a soft twat all your life. Yeah?' Arnold said punching his younger protégé on the shoulder.

Frank smiled.

'Righto.' Frank already had the next few hours planned out. This copper may be a criminal, he may be a horrible bloke hence he is being held in the cells, but Frank felt that everyone deserved second chances. If it wasn't for second chances, God knows where he would have been in life.

So, he was going to try and get him some food and maybe get him out to the shower.

The poor guy was half-dead already.

As Arnold left the yard, Frank stayed and lit a cigarette. He looked up at the night sky, stars becoming visible against the deep blue backdrop.

He exhaled his smoke, wondering how many people knew about this facility and what went on here. It was decribed as a 'Border Facility,' but Frank knew that there was something very, very wrong with what was happening here.

Part of him wanted to know more, despite being genuinely chilled to the core.

He threw his cigarette to the floor and headed back towards the 'A' block.

He opened the door and took a sharp intake of breath.

'Mr Wells.'

'Good… good evening Mr Wadham…' Frank spluttered.

'Are you not meant to be watching our… guest?' Wadham stated, his blue eyes boring into Frank.

'Of course, yeah, I was just-'

'-Smoking. Yes, I saw. Disgusting habit that.'

'Sorry, boss.'

Behind Wadham in black trousers and a white t-shirt was someone Frank only knew of as 'The Carver.'

'Open the door, Mr Wells,' Wadham said.

Frank obliged and they all entered the room.

Charlie was sitting on the floor, leaning against the wall in his usual position.

'Tie him up,' Wadham indicated to Frank.

Reticently, Frank followed the orders. He had a pair of handcuffs on his belt and he knew that there was a circular steel ring built into the stone floor.

The Carver pulled his own t-shirt over his head to reveal his torso, or indeed what was left of it.

There were cuts, grazes and scars. His surface skin was a smorgasbord of different colours and textures. Frank felt slightly nauseous as he clipped the handcuffs into place.

'We meet again, Charlie,' Wadham said. 'I need some answers from you this time, ole boy.'

The Carver pulled out a machete and one large carving knife of similar length. He started scraping the two instruments together.

Charlie smiled. His face was barely recognisable anyway.

'What were you doing in Temeraire Heights?' Wadham continued.

Silence.

The Carver moved closer; Charlie stayed stock still.

He was struck with two blows into his shoulder blades.

Blood poured from the two incisions, about an inch wide and Charlie yelped in pain.

'Like your old pal Glenn Beddle... this one knows about pain. How to inflict it. How to make it resonate, *fully*...' Wadham continued, as the knives struck again, this time slicing Charlie's torso, with two clean slashes along the ribs.

'What were you doing in Temeraire Heights, Charlie?' Wadham asked more forcefully.

The Carver was excited, his breath had quickened and his small round face revealed a smirk. The blood lust had begun.

'*I* have no need to keep you alive, Charlie. Sadly, there are other forces at work.' Wadham said, kneeling down to Charlie's face level, anxious to avoid getting blood on his dark grey suit.

Charlie lifted his head and launched himself, gripping Wadham's nose with his teeth.

It was Wadham's turn to yelp in pain, as Charlie managed to cling to his face for a good few seconds before intervention from his sidekick.

The Carver picked up a cloth and held it to his master's nose.

Wadham, infuriated, indicated to him to continue his work.

He twirled the blades in his hand and circled Charlie, who sat in a pool of crimson.

He sliced each arm four times in short, sharp movements along Charlie's upper arms.

The Carver stopped, awaiting instruction.

'What were you doing following me, Stone?!' Wadham cried, through the green and white tea towel he had fixed to his face.

Charlie laughed at the scene, despite the appalling nature of his own situation.

Wadham nodded once more at The Carver.

The Carver hesitated and looked over at Frank.

'Sir, I think…'

'You think what, Wells?' Wadham spat.

'I uh… think you're going to kill him…' Frank said softly.

Wadham removed the tea towel and grabbed the blade from the Carver.

He slashed hard and fast at Charlie's face.

The Carver pulled his master away and took the knife and the three men stood in silence, staring at the limp frame of Charlie Stone, who was slowly dying.

'Clean him up! Keep him alive! Alive!' Wadham shouted, as The Carver packed up his toolkit and he and Wadham exited the cell.

Frank looked at Charlie and wretched.

His eyes flitted around the cell. The only thing to use was the roll up mattress. He grabbed it and covered Charlie's arms and torso with it.

Frank ran out of the room and toward the small kitchenette that the men used along corridor 'A'.

Under the sink was a roll of J-cloths, previously untouched.

He grabbed them and ran back to tend to the rest of Charlie's wounds.

He was shivering and shaking, writhing on the floor. The mattress that engulfed him was rapidly turning claret.

Frank, despite treading a slightly nefarious line, had never killed anybody, or indeed watched anyone die.

He grabbed his phone from his pocket and with trembling hands began to dial Arnold.

There was no answer.

Charlie was cold and had passed out now. Frank was panicking.

He checked the one missed call he had, from 'Trev.'

Trev will know what to do, Frank thought to himself.

He rang the number back and it was immediately picked up.

'Hello?' came the voice aggressively on the other line.

'Hi, Trev. It's Frank.'

'Frankie boy, how you doing?' the voice became friendlier.

'I've been better-'

'-Talk to me, what's up?'

'You remember how you know how to keep someone alive?'

'Well, kinda depends on the situation?'

'I need help now! I got a fella dying on me here, and I need to keep him alive.'

'Fuck me, Frank, what have you got yourself into?'

'This fucked up job working security for Wolfire. They're into some dark shit, Trev. But I need the guy now. This one's fading on me.'

'I see. Who is it?'

'Some copper that they brought into the facility last night.'

'Oh really. A copper?'

'Yeah, Charlie Stone or something. Listen, we ain't got time for that now.'

'Charlie? I'll come right now. What's happened to him?'

'He's been carved up, bad…'

'Pressure to the wounds, Frankie!'

'Yeah, there's a few of them... that's the problem.'

The phone went dead.

****

Robbie's phone flashed a text from Trev.

Urgent, come now.

Robbie looked at the dishevelled naked woman on the bed. He crawled off of her body and started putting his clothes on rapidly.

'I have got to go,' he said into the air. A look of relief washed over Mayya's face, as she started putting her underwear back on quietly.

'OK, baby,' she whispered.

Robbie was already out of the door, with his phone in hand and hoodie up over his head.

'Don't slam the-' Maya said softly, but it was too late as the door crashed into the frame and Robbie bolted for his car.

As he started the engine and sped away, he dialled Trev's number on his mobile.

'Yeah, Trev, what's up? I was on the job, son.'

'Don't worry about that. We have a situation. Your pal, Charlie. He's been cut up bad. Kidnapped. We need to bust him out.'

'Oh, shit,' Robbie perked up on the other end of the line. 'You packed the tools?'

'Yes, boss. The bigger ones. I'll be ready in five.'

'Righto!'

****

Frank cradled the copper in his arms. He felt like he was holding his whole body together.

He had worked with Trev for several years and knew if he needed help, Trev would know what to do.

Frank believed that Trev would track the coordinates of the phone, but he wasn't sure how the doctor would be able to get through security.

Frank quickly dialled the number of the facility and got through to reception.

'Hi, its Frank, security. Listen, I have a doctor coming in, it's urgent, right? He needs to get through as otherwise we have someone here who is going to die...'

'What's the er...doctor's name, sir...' came the voice on the other end of the line.

'I don't know, but you need to let him through!'

'Oh, OK sir, I think he's here now...' there was a sound of movement and shouting, 'Doctor, coming through!' before the line went dead.

Frank waited quietly and hopefully to Charlie's breathing which remained terribly light, but audible.

There was a loud gunshot and then the sound of two voices once more.

'Frank?'

'In here!'

Big Robbie came bustling through the door with his friend, Trevor.

'Jesus…' Robbie looked at Charlie.

'We need to get him straight in the van,' Trevor said.

'Right,' Robbie loaded two more cartridges into his sawn-off shotgun and stood guard while the other two carried Charlie's body.

'Careful with him, eh?' Trevor said looking at Frank, who riding on a wave of adrenaline nodded.

A loud alarm pierced the otherwise silent night sky.

'Careful, but quick. There'll be a private army here any minute,' Robbie said, leading the way through the courtyard.

The lads followed with the body wrapped up, seeping, with blood on their hands.

A security guard with a truncheon and a small pistol burst through the door in front of them.

'Thank you for getting the door, now get on your knees, before I take your head off,' Robbie said calmly, pointing the sawn-off at the guard's terrified face.

The guard dropped his gun and did as he was told. Trevor bent down and picked up the pistol as they ran past and into the reception area.

'Any more of you pricks in there?' Robbie shouted, bursting into reception and surveying the scene.

Luckily for them the coast was clear as Robbie led on through the front of the building and to an old Ford transit van that was parked across the front entrance.

Robbie stood guard as Trev opened the back doors which were fastened together with a padlock.

The men placed Charlie in there and Trevor jumped inside to tend to him. Frank padlocked the van behind them.

'Right you're up front with me, Frankie. I have a feeling this is going to get fruity.'

Frank smiled. He was terrified and excited at the same time.

As they jumped into the front seats of the van, three black cars pulled up, two with sirens on the top of their cars.

'Quick, Frank!' Trev shouted from the back as the engine roared to life.

'Ere, shoot their tyres.' Robbie said, as Frank grabbed a sawn-off shotgun from the footwell.

The weight surprised Frank but he held it out the window and aimed at the front tyre of the first car.

He squeezed the trigger just as the van sped off. The shot hit the wheel, denting it. A piece of shrapnel flew off and pierced the tyre which slowly started to deflate.

'Good job!' Robbie said, beaming from ear to ear.

'Mate, drive sensibly!' Trevor bellowed from the back.

He slowed slightly, and one of the cars sped up behind the van.

With the second shot from the gun, Frank fired at the car, this time piercing the bonnet, causing smoke to rise from the engine.

The car stopped, thinking better of their proposed chase.

The van came to the end of the long dirt track and within three turnings had pulled onto the deserted M20 motorway and was heading back to Trevor's flat in Folkestone.

20

The phone was ringing.
Maddie looked at it and ignored it.
It stopped and she looked at it again. She sighed and turned it onto silent.
She carried on colouring at her desk.
The light from the screen flashed on, a message… please Maddie, I just want to see how you are.
Maddie begins to cry.
Her Mum enters from another room, sees Maddie upset and picks the phone up, turns it off.

'Listen son, I'll bet you now… a ton… Tottenham don't win the league…'
Everything was blurry, everything was sore.
'Nah, come on. Put your money where your mouth is!'
His eyes tried to open, but it wasn't happening. No energy.
'Chelsea? No chance. Not consistent enough. Not until they buy Declan Rice off you lot.'
Finally, a crack of light through his eyelids, piercing.
'Here he is! Ere Char, Char wake up.'
Charlie could feel the force of a bear paw shoving him into life.
'Gently, mate,' came another voice.
'Oh yeah, sorry.'
Charlie's eyes opened. He could see three figures around him, or so he thought.

The light streamed in from the window. He looked down at his frame and things came further into focus.

He was heavily bandaged across his arms and torso. He was wearing his favourite pair of jeans still; they had been painted a shade of red by his recent experiences.

'How you doing?' came a voice. Charlie looked to his left to see Trevor, Robbie's mate.

'Yeah…' Charlie croaked.

Trevor passed him a small glass of water. Charlie swallowed it down.

'You are going to feel like shit for a while, pal,' Trevor continued.

With that, Charlie tried to move his body in the makeshift bed. He was like a pile of bones, yet everything ached.

'Hm. Maddie?' Charlie uttered.

'Erm… don't know mate,' Trevor said, unaware of who Maddie was.

Charlie sighed. He remembered back to his experience and shuddered.

'Give me my phone…'

Charlie focused and punched in the digits.

The phone was picked up immediately.

'Charlie?!'

'Tara…?'

'Charlie! You're OK! Oh, Charlie… where are you?' Tara said excitedly.

Charlie looked around. He vaguely recognised Trevor's flat and saw the church tower near

Central Station from the window.

'Folkestone.'

Trevor shot Charlie a glance and shook his head. Charlie furrowed his brow, angry at the intrusion.

'I'll be home soon…'

'Yeah, maybe a few days,' Trevor said, loud enough for Tara to hear down the line.

'Who's that?' Tara asked.

'Don't worry. Have you heard from Maddie?' Charlie asked.

There was a pause.

'No Charlie. But we have court in two days time.'

'Great… and the baby?'

'Everything is fine here. I'm good, Charlie. What about you?' Tara asked.

Trevor intimated to put the phone down.

'I'll be home soon. I love you.'

'I love-'

Charlie put the phone down.

'What's the problem?' Charlie asked, angry that his romantic encounter had been interrupted.

'You very nearly bled out, Charlie. There are some people who don't just want you dead, they want you to suffer. If they want to get at you, who knows what they'll do, eh?' Robbie said.

Charlie knew he was right. Maddie and Tara would be the next targets, especially since he had escaped.

'I need to get back to see her…. I need to protect

her.' Charlie said, shifting his position in bed.

'Relax, Char. You need to get better. She'll be OK.'

'Oh really? Like I am?' Charlie said angrily.

'She's a civilian, pal. It's different. You were talking about a baby?'

'She's pregnant.'

Robbie smiled.

'There's rules to this shit, Charlie. She'll be fine.'

Charlie thought about Robbie's words. He wasn't convinced. They had targeted Maddie before, what's to say they wouldn't do it again?

Charlie spent the rest of the day sitting up in Trevor's makeshift bed, trying to regain strength and movement in his limbs and trying to keep down water and small morsels of food.

The encounter with The Carver had taken its toll on him; he did not feel the same.

A darkness pervaded his mind. He wanted to be optimistic, yet he was losing the light.

The world was brutal, it was broken and nothing Charlie Stone could do would change that.

'The facility?' Charlie said, trying to conserve as much energy as possible.

'It's up on the other side of Ashford, in a large field surrounded by more fields. It's actually built into a valley, so you can't see it until you're there, if you know what I mean. Called the Sevington Inland Border Facility,' Frank divulged.

'Border Facility? It's not...'

Charlie trailed off.

'Yeah, we gathered. There's more going on there than the public know about, that's for sure.' Trevor said.

Frank continued, 'Yeah its supposed to be a processing facility for immigrants who come across the Channel. I saw a lot of people... a real mix, you know?'

Trevor and Charlie looked up as the Frank fumbled the right words, not wanting to be offensive.

'...Some who don't look like immigrants?' Charlie finished the sentence off for him.

'Yeah, exactly,' Frank agreed.

'There's a mix, for definite. One theory is that they are trying out different vaccines for the virus,' added Trev.

Charlie nodded. 'Something like that.' He shifted in his bed.

'So, come on Char. Let the dog see the rabbit. What happened to you?' Robbie asked, sitting backwards on the only available chair.

'I'm trying to remember what went on... I had left the pub in Sandgate. I was going to go home and saw a black Mercedes. I tailed it to Temeraire Heights, which is where Wadham and Gibson's prostitution ring started. I thought it was all shut down now. It wasn't. I also thought Wadham was locked up...'

'Well, he isn't anymore. Is he the guy who did this to you?' Trevor asked.

'No. He has a sidekick. "The Carver".' Robbie sniggered at the pseudonym.

'Well, he will be the first one we go after,' Robbie said.

Trevor rubbed his chin and looked at Charlie, who was staring out of the window.

'We need to get back in that facility,' Charlie said.

'That's going to be tricky…' Trev followed up, but something in his voice made the other men believe he was in fact entertaining the idea.

'There's some activity in there that's completely off-grid, totally classified. There was this door… a black door… and at times you could just hear whimpering, wailing…', commented Frank. Charlie looked away. Despite his experiences with The Carver, it was this that truly struck a nerve with him. Charlie knew from experience what these people were capable of. Charlie was a soldier in this battle between good and evil. The fight is fair and Charlie knew the rules. These people, Wood, Wadham, they don't play by the same rules that the rest of society do.

'Leave it with me. I'll see what I can get together. Let things die down for a few days and we can see what we can do,' Trev said.

Robbie nodded.

Trevor's phone buzzed in Charlie's hand.

Don't forget, we need to prepare for court on Thursday x x x

'Oh, Christ. You're going to have to get me home,' Charlie said raising himself from the bed. Everything ached. But his spirits were higher. He had been adamant he was going to die in that cell, at the hands of Paul Wadham.

Yet he was still alive and he had another chance for vengeance. For justice.

21

Tara was anxious as she noticed the WhatsApp was read, but not responded to.

What had happened to him? She knew he was troubled, but going out all night… his behaviour had become all too erratic… too dangerous.

Her phone lit up.

I'll be home in ten. I love you x x x

I love you too x x x,

She relaxed and returned immediately to the kitchen to put the kettle on.

Her movements were slow and laboured, but despite that she wasn't suffering too badly. She placed her hand on her swollen stomach and felt a sense of pride, that she was going to be a mother.

The mother of Charlie Stone's child.

She would love and nurture the baby and make sure it didn't suffer the way its father suffered.

Neglect and violence were Charlie's parents as a young boy. Tara knew that Charlie was determined to give his son the starts that he never had.

Tara just needed to make sure that Charlie could stay safe and crack this Wood case once and for all, before the baby was born.

Despite her optimistic outlook, she knew that

this was unlikely.

As she waited for the kettle to boil, there was something in the sky above their garden.

She didn't have her glasses on, but she noticed the whirring propellers and bright blue light. A drone.

Her phone lit up once more, a withheld number. She sighed, toying with whether to answer it. Probably some company wanting money she didn't have.

Tara ignored it.

The bubbles in the kettle become larger. The water roared and the phone came to life again.

A withheld number once more.

'Yes, hello?' she answered with a sigh, feeling a kick from the little rascal inside of her. She winced, as the voice came on the other line.

'You all right there, Tara? Looks like you're struggling?' It was a friendly, male voice. One she recognised.

'Who is this please?'

The drone moved in the sky, nearer to the house.

'Things have changed, eh? Since the school. Maths department do's and having one too many drinks, eh?'

Tara felt her anxiety and fear rise as the drone came to the patio door at her eye level.

'Ah, still beautiful. Even with his baby in you. I must say though, for someone shacked up with Charlie Stone, the security is surprisingly lax, T...'

T?

The penny suddenly dropped.

'Troy? Is that you?'

Silence.

'What do you want?' Tara said, tears of frustration forming in her eyes.

'Just some friendly advice, T. He's trouble, that man of yours, and he has upset the wrong people. But I think you know that. You can't keep coming to his aid, hoping he's going to change and it's all going to be OK. It's not.'

'Wh-'

'It's not going to be OK for Charlie Stone and I think you know it, deep in your heart, Tara.'

The tears came now, loud and ferocious.

'But, I-'

'-Love him? It passes, T. You deserve safety. Happiness. Security for your baby. Don't you want that? Don't you want your love requited?'

Tara continued to cry.

'Leave me alone, Troy!'

'Yes, Charlie's home anyway. Think about it, Tara.'

The phone line went dead and Tara heard a tentative key in the front door.

She went to it and saw her love enter and fall into her arms.

'Jesus, Charlie!'

She held him, shocked by the scabs that had formed the marks... the scars.

'It's OK. I'm OK,' Charlie said softly.

Tara helped Charlie up the stairs to the bedroom.

He was in acute pain and Tara could tell.

She lay him down under the covers, and went down to fetch painkillers, water and to start some food on the hob.

She pulled a tin of chicken soup from the larder and checked for the drone in the garden.

There was nothing there.

She battled with Troy's easy, confident voice suggesting to her a different life. A life she so desperately wanted. And the man she loved upstairs, battered, bruised and burdened.

It was no contest for her.

When Tara returned to Charlie with the provisions, he was half-asleep. She nudged him awake and urged him to eat and drink.

He obliged, not realising until now, how depleted his reserves were.

Tara watched Charlie fall in and out of fitful sleep.

It was now Tuesday evening and he had been home resting for six hours.

She wanted him to sleep overnight if possible, and that gave them a day tomorrow before they were due in court.

Charlie needed to be somewhere near his best, so he turned off his bedside lamp and closed his eyes.

****

Charlie stirred as sunlight filtered through the blinds.

He reached for the alarm clock on the floor by the bed, which read 6.03am.

He had two messages from Trev, which he quickly read:

I know you have things on, but I have a plan for the facility.

Contact me in a few days or when you're feeling better.

Charlie felt Tara's warmth beside him. She was lightly snoring and he reached over to hug her.

He felt her stomach, burgeoning now with the weight of his first boy. He smiled to himself, he couldn't hide his pride. He checked the calendar on his phone for a due date which was April 4th. The time would fly.

Charlie rose from the bed quietly, his limbs slowly coming to life after a long slumber. He pulled on some clean joggers and jumper and left Tara to rest, heading downstairs to put the kettle on.

He looked in the mirror and was pleased with what he saw.

He was scarred, cut and bruised but better than he expected.

He made a cup of steaming black coffee and analysed the letter that sat on the mantelpiece from Hastings County Court.

Tomorrow was D-day for him, make or break. His heart yearned to see his daughter again.

After his coffee, there was still no stirring from upstairs so he went out into the bright morning and started speed walking.

His limbs were still achey and his body told him to stop immediately, so he slowly limped around to Willesborough rec, before heading through the cemetery and out towards the church on Hythe Road.

The walk cleared his head and made him feel better, the air revitalising the lungs, filling him with energy.

His wounds had been dressed expertly by Trevor, like glue holding his frame together. He was fragile, but he would repair.

On the route back around, he decided to stop for another coffee at the Willesborough cafe. As he entered, he witnessed three army vehicles speeding past along Hythe Road and towards the motorway.

An old man in front of him turned at the growling of the engine, then nodded to himself.

'What's happening there?' Charlie asked.

'Heading down to Dover. They've closed the docks so it's bedlam. People scared about the virus, so France closed the border. You not seen the motorway?'

Charlie shook his head. He hadn't. In fact, he had no idea what had been going on.

He got his coffee to take away and walked up to the bridge over the M20.

It was like something from a dystopian movie.

Lines of trucks filled the southbound carriage as far back as he could see towards Maidstone, and into the distance towards Folkestone. The central lane had been kept clear for police and other vehicles to move through, and the northbound carriages were deserted.

Charlie felt anxious. Wood's chilling premonition seemed to be taking hold.

Charlie grabbed a paper from the BP garage and started for home.

He came in quietly through the back door, so as not to wake Tara, but he could hear movement in the front room. Shuffling.

He walked in and saw her place her phone on the arm of the chair. She looked up and smiled at him, red faced and bleary eyed.

'What's up, sweet?' he asked, sitting beside her, eyeing the phone.

'Nothing, it's nothing. Just hormones with this little one,' she said, pointing at her tummy.

'Hm.'

'How are you feeling?' she said, wiping her nose with an old tissue.

'Good. I mean, you know… better.'

Tara smiled and put her hand in his.

She steeled herself and went to get the folder she had been creating, labelling and colour coding since she had witness of the court date.

'Right,' she said. 'Get comfortable.'

22

Thursday arrived and Tara drove down to Hastings Crown Court, with Charlie as her passenger.

Luckily, they didn't have to engage with the M20 and were in fact going in completely the opposite direction, so the traffic was merciful.

It was an hour's drive through the marshlands of south Kent, up towards historic Rye in East Sussex, then on to Winchelsea and eventually into the sprawling town of Hastings.

Another traditional seaside town that had luckily benefitted from a coastal regeneration, with mini-golf, adventure playgrounds and fairground rides along the front.

Due to this, a number of independent boutique-style shops had opened up, selling upcycled furniture and artisan coffee.

This quarter of the town was pleasant, otherwise it would be old 'Cashino's,' dilapidated ice cream shops and eighties-style kid's arcades.

Charlie pondered where it ranked in the top ten of south-eastern seaside towns. His experience had taught him that many of the council's had done an excellent job at selling a vision of certain coastal places, yet not addressed the real issues of the place. He wondered whether living in Hastings would be like this; a lovely place to visit, but aggravating to live in.

Either way, he surmised, it was somewhere in

between Folkestone and Brighton in the top ten, but definitely up there.

'I think it's just up here on the left,' Tara mused, analysing the sat-nav.

Charlie felt a wave of anxiety flood him.

He reached into his pocket and pulled out a handkerchief for his suit pocket. Deep blue to match his grey suit. The one he hadn't worn for several years and was significantly tighter than he remembered.

Tara pulled the car to a halt.

'You OK?' she asked looking over at him.

'Hmm,' Charlie returned, aggressively opening the car door.

He got out and went around to help Tara, who was wearing an emerald green dress, made of some stretchy material.

'It's going to go well, Charlie. Just relax and be yourself.'

Charlie wasn't OK and he wasn't sure that it was going to go well.

As much as he had assisted in bringing men and women to criminal justice many times over, this was different. Family Court.

It was never a fair starting point. Ever. The system was appallingly skewed towards the mother.

It was the elephant in the judicial system's living room, refusing to move forward, or to adapt to modern times.

It was the cause of many men, good men,

turning from their families into darkness, and some ultimately deciding that staying in a world, and a system that is so corrupt, was no longer worth it.

When he was married to Jo, Charlie was happy to assume the collective narrative of the mainstream media. That separated men were not interested in their children, that their infidelities proved their lack of commitment to their families, that in fact, the children were better off with limited or no contact with their fathers.

He would watch Spiderman and Batman traverse bridges, Houses of Parliament, Trafalgar Square and protest, thinking very little of their actions. Swallowing the narrative that they were desperate criminals, causing unrest.

Well, he now knew that desperation. The sadness and the longing caused by homes devastated by divorce.

You can retrieve a child's esteem if the parent's work together, but if you don't, the battleground will always take its toll.

Like all wars, it is the innocent who suffer most.

Sadly, Jo was not prepared to call a ceasefire. She only wanted revenge, rage and retribution.

There would be no white flag, despite repeated attempts. She would not be challenged.

Challenge was met with fury in pure draconian fashion.

Off with their heads, and Charlie's was on the block.

'Place all your items in the box please sir,' the guard said, as he ushered Tara and then Charlie through the metal detector.

Charlie wondered how many times he had been through these moments, sitting on the other side of the court room. Today, it was him on trial. Facing judgment.

Charlie collected his things and went through to the waiting room outside Court Two, where his case was being heard first.

He could sense bodies moving in front of him and he stopped.

The voices stopped, but Charlie could make out Jo's mop of blonde curls up the stairs beyond him.

Her deep, husky voice started again, this time as a whisper and Charlie made his way back down the stairs, intimating to Tara to sit somewhere else.

'Hello, Charles,' came a voice from behind him.

Charlie sighed.

He turned and made his way back up the stairs, to be met by Jo's father, John Kelly.

He held out his hand and Charlie took it, staring him straight in the eyes.

Behind him, Charlie noticed Jo's mother hobbling about. She suffered from a rather unfortunate case of Kyphosis, where the back hunches. As her age increased, so did the issue. She made no eye contact with Charlie and despite her difficulties and general unpleasantness, Charlie felt sorry for her.

He remembered back to April 2009, when Charlie and Jo accompanied her parents on a trip to Brittany. On the boat, Jo's mother asked Charlie to play cards with her. As they sat and talked, she asked him questions about his own mother: 'does she have Charlie's best interest at heart? Why do you think she does the things she does? Is she happy with his new relationship?'

In addition to this, she followed up with comments such as, 'I am always here for you to talk to, hopefully this is a new chapter and a new start, you'll be surely spending more time with us now rather than down in Kent…'

Charlie knew enough about people to know there was an ulterior motive here. His back was up with her from the start.

Then the Foie Gras incident that Christmas Day in 2013 proved his suspicions right…

Beyond her, Charlie saw Jo's new boyfriend. A pale-faced, dark-haired slip of a man, looking overtly at Charlie with a wry smile.

Charlie went back down to find Tara.

'What was that about?' she asked.

'God knows…'

'I mean, she is trying to screw you at court, making out you're the devil incarnate, and her Dad is shaking your hand?' Tara whispered.

'Indeed. That's sadly how it works in his corporate world, I guess,' Charlie said, taking up her hand and holding it tightly.

They took a seat near the courtroom and waited. Charlie felt a blurry and peculiar inner peace. There was no time here, just the mercy of the officials. There was no phone signal either, just Charlie, his girlfriend and the fate of his only child.

He knew that Jo was likely to win due to the unfair court system, and he knew that he would probably be forced, when he did lose, to pay Jo's court fees of around twelve thousand pounds.

This made him feel sick, despite the fact that he knew it would be split into manageable payments. He didn't owe it. She had brought a fake case in answer to Charlie's request to see more of his daughter, and Charlie would be stung with the bill.

Eventually they were called.

As Tara and Charlie went to open the large, wooden door of the court, a small woman in a business suit stood in front of them.

'I am afraid, Mr Stone, that your request to bring a McKenzie friend into the courtroom has been refused.'

Tara looked forlorn.

Charlie hugged her.

'Don't worry,' he said smiling, he knew it wouldn't affect his fate anyway.

'Good luck,' she whispered.

Charlie though was already through the doors, and ready to take his seat.

'So, Mr Stone... let me get this right... you

brought a CT04 against... uh... Miss Kelly... for breach of a court order created in 2015...'

'Yes, your honour.'

'...And then Miss Kelly... you counterclaimed against Mr Stone for... well in effect, you have applied for a non-molestation order against Mr Stone it would appear?'

Jo's barrister rose.

'Your honour...'

'Wait a minute, please,' The judge replied.

'Sorry, your honour,' she said, sitting back down. Jo's barrister was a stern woman from her demeanour, in a blue business suit and impatient to get this across the line for her client and no doubt, her career.

'I have a written statement regarding the events surrounding the case from each of you,' the judge said acknowledging Jo and Charlie, who both sat on opposite sides of the room, Charlie a row behind his ex-wife.

'An initial statement from Mr Stone and a response from Miss Kelly?'

The individuals both nodded.

'I have read both statements prior to the case and I have to say there are some issues that require clarification, in particular on the respondent's part.'

Jo shifted in her seat and her barrister sat eyes wide, ears pricked.

'In this response to Mr Stone's statement it is claimed that you were a "victim of domestic abuse…"' Jo nodded eagerly.

'However, I can't see any evidence of you filing a report or taking any action during your marriage, is that right, Miss Kelly?'

The two women conferred together, before the barrister stood up.

'Your honour, like many women who find themselves in this situation, Miss Kelly didn't realise that she was a victim of domestic abuse while she was in the relationship. It was only after the marriage had ended and she had the opportunity to discuss the situation with other people that she realised she felt isolated and alone. She does say that in her statement.'

The judge fingered the documents that were in front of him.

'Hm. I see. However, feeling isolated and alone in a marriage does not equate to domestic abuse and as you say… violence, does it?' he continued.

There was further, more frantic discussion between the two before the barrister rose once more.

'Sometimes, your honour, it is unclear how the respondent was damaging to my client's life, at the time, but in hindsight, the activities that he… engaged with, were abusive towards her.'

'Yet, there is no evidence of this. Can you elaborate?'

'Well… an example could be where he used to 'tickle' my client or even pinch her…'

The judge's eyebrows rose and for the first time he looked up from the page and directly at the barrister.

'What… like *playfighting?'*

'No… like abuse!' retorted the barrister somewhat enraged.

'Hm. Yet these allegations are made… two years after separation and divorce?' the judge continued calmly.

'Your honour, he called her *'a cock-loving chubbster!'* the Barrister blurted desperately.

The judge looked once again at the papers in front of him.

'Yes, I saw that. In an email, it says right here…' the judge pored over the papers while the barrister sat down.

'Give me a few moments here, to collect my thoughts and re-read these lengthy documents.'

There was a stunned silence in the room. Charlie felt some hope. It was the first time since his divorce he felt that events had been looked at transparently and objectively.

His whole raison d'etre was torn apart by a bad marriage and a worse divorce. He was ripped away from his only child. He was tricked into renting a property in Folkestone, under the premise Maddie would be near, would be accessible.

He lost his driving license due to her. He left in the night to stop the two arguing and Jo called the police. He had his car key on him and she had told them that he intended to drive.

As much as civvies believe the police can get away with anything, and they look after their own, that was not always the case.

Charlie had tried and tried to make communications amicable and friendly. When this had been rebuffed, Tara had tried to smooth things over and take control to make things work. Nothing worked. One-minute Jo was happy to communicate with her; the next minute it had to be Charlie.

Jo was the ringleader of a cruel circus and unless you were prepared to be brutalised into submission and submit to her whims, you were out.

Finally, she was now in breach of the court order and refusing to let Maddie, their daughter, visit her father.

Through all of this, Charlie had suffered the blows and been told he was the monster. That it was all his fault.

Neglect. Violence. Silence. The Jo Kelly way.

For the first time in years, there was a brief crack of light.

'Mr Stone, I would like to invite you now to comment on this… situation please,' the judge said.

Charlie stood; the judge eyed him carefully.

He was wearing his grey suit jacket and underneath he wore his Fathers for Justice t-shirt which read, Equal Parents, Equal Love.

'Thank you, your honour. I submitted the documents to court because I have been prevented from seeing my child. This is on the premise that I am dangerous and at risk of causing her harm. My line of work has been unpredictable and has directly affected Maddie, however this has now been resolved-'

'-Can you explain what you mean please, there are many police officers who have children, Mr Stone?' the judge asked.

'Of course. The criminal who put Maddie in danger is deceased. We have moved to a new location in a separate town which is far safer and secure. Most importantly however, I am no longer in the police force, which is where all of this stemmed from.'

The judge nodded and scribbled on his paper.

'The respondent has focused her entire counter-claim on me personally, and our marriage which ended years ago. This suggests to me that her focus is not currently on Maddie's wellbeing.'

The eyebrows of the judge raised once more.

'I will be the first one to admit that there are some things that have been said that are not ideal. We are dealing with emotions that run high, especially when the custody of a child is concerned. Sadly, your honour, all I want is to see my daughter. I think it's appalling that a mother has the right to prevent a child from seeing their father. The mother and father divorced, neither of us divorced our child.'

The judge raised a hand. He was impossible to read, so Charlie quietened and sat back down.

'No, stay standing Mr Stone. But I understand this is emotive for you, clearly, but please hurry along to the point now.'

'OK, the point is that I want what is in the best interest of my daughter. If you ask her, and Ms Kelly even admits in her statement, that she wants a relationship with her father, so why has this been prevented? Finally, I wanted to provide some further insight into why I think these allegations and claims have arisen, so long after our marriage. If I may refer you to page three of the additional documents, there are two quotations from Ms Kelly which I think highlight the motivation and where this continued animosity has risen from and form the basis of this unrelenting assault:

"On Thursday you threatened that you had taken legal action and you insinuated I may lose Maddie. For that I can never forgive you." – Ms Kelly via email, 23rd November 2014.

"I wish I never had to deal with you again for anything. One day u r sickly sweet, the next u r demanding and controlling. U r difficult. U think u have been amicable- what a joke. u r beyond ludicrous. The bottom line- u were an awful husband. Controlling, manipulative, selfish, irrisponsible, difficult and at times downright horrible. The fact

that u r surprised I left u and said I didn't love u anymore r testament to the fact that u r oblivious to how u behave. Be clear however. I am in control with regards to Maddie - end of story." – Ms Kelly, 23 dec 2014

A non-molestation order or injunction is required when a party is 'at risk of being a victim of domestic abuse or violence from the other party in the case arising from a family relationship between you and the other party.'

I don't and have not resided with the applicant for nearly four years. I have not seen the applicant for months now as I have deliberately extricated myself from any situation involving her for fear of further accusation, acrimony and allegation.

I have tried very hard to keep from airing all of our laundry. However, these direct quotations should provide some insight into the truth of the situation.'

Charlie sat down and felt immediately relieved. He had no idea how the axe would fall, but he had spoken honestly and from the heart.

He had not fabricated events or tried to sugar-coat his own misdemeanours.

The Judge took off his glasses and prepared to speak.

'This seems fairly clear to me. Mr Stone, you have made it very apparent that your only interest is in seeing your daughter. It appears that contact has not been allowed on a number of occasions and I find this directly against the interests of the child.

It is obvious, as with any break-up, there has been animosity and unpleasantness on both sides. I think it is important to note here, Ms Kelly that this has been a two-way street-'

'-But, your honour,' the barrister interjected, but was met with short thrift by the swift rise of the judge's right hand.

'As I was saying, the bitterness and unpleasantness is a two-way street and needs to stop. I can see that Mr Stone has written in his witness statement that he acknowledges this, and has made some amends to do this. I need to see this on both sides moving forward.

As such, I will not grant the non-molestation order. There is no evidence of domestic abuse or violence historically and it looks very unlikely that there will be. Ms Kelly, you and I both know you don't need protection from Mr Stone, he just wants to see his daughter.'

Jo's head fell and the tears started to fall.

'What is very important is that contact starts again between Mr Stone and his daughter with immediate effect. What is between you should not be allowed to affect the young girl... Madeleine... in question here.'

'But-'

'Sit down, you have said quite enough now thank you!' the judge boomed at the barrister's final interjection.

'On the contrary, I would urge you, Ms Kelly, to take the advice I give you and try and build positive relationships here, for the sake of your own daughter. There is no doubt what has occurred between you and Mr Stone has been somewhat… grisly… however the past is what it is. It can be made better.'

With that the judge rose from his seat, Charlie exhaled pure relief and Jo slumped on the table in front of her and wept.

23

On the drive home, Charlie organised to meet his mother with Tara at an old pub in Icklesham. It had beautiful views of the Kent countryside and Charlie was pleased to have his nearest and dearest around him, after a week of physical and emotional turmoil. His body seemed to ride the recovery process whilst he was in the courtroom, but now after the ecstasy and elation, his aches and pains were returning.

'You must be delighted,' his mother said, looking at the menu. 'After all the stress and the worry about the legal fees…'

'It really has taken some preparation, but to know that Charlie's name is clear and he can breathe again…'

'Absolutely. And the right thing is being done, when in fact you were very worried it wouldn't…'

The voices provided the background noise but Charlie was in a daze.

He couldn't quite describe the emotions he was feeling. There was a palpable relief about Maddie. She could come down now, and hopefully more often. The details would be battered out at a subsequent hearing to be determined, but there was a funny gnawing in his stomach.

'To think she could try and get us to pay… for

her fees! And she knows that we have a baby on the way…'

Charlie was overjoyed that he didn't have to pick up a tab clocked up by his ex-wife. A tab she had created in an attempt to destroy him. Yet, that still didn't bring him a sense of joy.

'I can't believe that is actually allowed…'

'Well, the argument is if she wins and gets the non-mol, then it's his fault that she had to pay the fees in the first place…'

'Still, it seems a bit unfair…'

'It is unfair, mum. The whole thing is deeply unfair.' Charlie cut through the conversation.

'Well, it's a good thing, you won then, eh?' his mother said with a smile.

'Nobody wins, mum.'

The three sat in silence, briefly sensing Charlie's temperamental mood.

'Are you OK, Charlie? I thought you would be happier?' Tara spoke softly.

He paused.

'I mean, I am pleased with the outcome. It vindicates me, us. It proves that we weren't mad, that we were trying our best for Maddie and we can go back to being an integral part of her life, as we wanted to. It's just…it's a shame it came to this. That Jo felt she had to do it. And I'm sad for her. I feel great sadness. She was in floods of tears and I think when the verdict came, she realised the gravity of what she had done. At least I hope she did and it wasn't just the tears of sadness. Her family, my family. All of the innocent she had embroiled in her web. And for what?'

'Control, Charlie.' his mum said, finishing her drink in one.

Charlie nodded and went back to his drink and daze while his mum and girlfriend continued to make small talk across the table.

Charlie checked his phone and it was 1.10pm. The food had arrived and he was keen to get home and back to normality as soon as possible.

There was a case to solve, a facility to infiltrate and preparations for the arrival of Maddie at some stage soon.

His phone rang so he went outside to take it.

'Ello son! How are you getting on?'

'All right Rob, yeah good, good and you?' Charlie replied.

'Yeah, you know. Same old shit. Becky kicked me out again…'

'Oh right, what's happened?'

'Long story mate, but either way I'm staying in the Burstin and it ain't looking good. But anyway, what you been up to, I haven't spoken to you in a couple of days?'

'Well, recovering primarily. And I had that court case today…'

'Oh, shit, sorry mate, completely forgot. How did you get on?'

'Well, good if I'm honest. Better than I could have expected really.'

'Blinder! So that old slag is gonna back off then?' Robbie said guffawing to himself.

'Yeah mate, something like that.'

'Well, how's about you take me to that posh gym of yours this afternoon? I could go down the Burstin, but I'm worried what I'll catch in there. Plus, the bird who runs it is a stroppy cow. Can't have her seeing me in my speedos…'

'Firstly, you aren't coming anywhere with me in speedos, pal. This isn't France! But yeah, get some appropriate swimwear and I'll meet you up there.'

'What you saying, 2.30pm?'

'Sure thing. See you there, Rob.'

Charlie went back to the table and finished his drink. Their food was finished, so Charlie picked up the bill. Mercifully, it was far smaller than it could have been, had things have gone differently today.

They said goodbye to Charlie's mum and got in the car.

'Take me home please, I'm knackered and the baby is kicking me senseless,' Tara said, rubbing underneath her ribs.

The third trimester was certainly taking its toll on her petite frame.

'No worries, I'm going to go to the gym, if that's OK?'

'Of course,' Tara said, half asleep already.

Charlie saw Tara into the house and resisted the temptation to crawl into the warm pit beside her.

His gym kit was ready, so he grabbed the bag and got back in the car.

Fifteen minutes later he was greeted by Robbie's big bald frame outside the gym doors.

'All right son!' he said pulling Charlie in for his trademark bear hug.

'Come on then,' Charlie said, heading in and towards the reception area.

As Charlie went and waited to sign his friend in, Robbie had taken a brief look at the security set up, noticed no person was actually present, and vaulted the metal barriers.

'Mate, there is no need…' Charlie said forlornly, but Robbie was off, around the corner and heading towards the changing rooms.

Charlie took a deep breath, did a double check to make sure no-one had seen, and then signed in with his pass.

Once he arrived, Robbie was already in pants.

'Here, Char… how do these lockers work?'

'Well Robbie, they need a pass to open and lock them. Not so clever now, eh?'

Robbie's brow furrowed.

'It's all right, I'll just use yours.'

Charlie took a deep breath and started to get changed, careful not to disturb the dressings on his upper body. Charlie knew he wouldn't be able to do any form of weights, but he hoped he could jog or get on the elliptical, maybe.

They both trained in their own different ways. Charlie went straight to cardio, while Robbie hit the weights.

Charlie wasn't sure, but Robbie seemed like the type of guy who barely used a gym, but when he did, he could hit some of the heaviest weights and crush them. He may be in pieces the next day, but as long as he looked like the toughest guy in there, he wouldn't worry about that.

After about half an hour, Robbie began to get restless.

'Come on mate, let's get on the punchbags!' he said, smiling like a kid wanting to go to the park with his dad.

Charlie told Robbie to go ahead while he ran a couple more kilometres.

In fairness, Charlie enjoyed the boxing session.

'I used to box a bit when I was younger, Char. Thinking about getting back into it…' Robbie's large fist thudded into the bag.

'Why not? It's going to keep you fit and keep you out of trouble.'

'Yeah, I think I might. Gives me some space away from her indoors too…'

'So, what is going on with Becky then?' Charlie said, taking his turn on the bag and thundering an upper cut into the centre of it.

'You know how it is, pal. I'm just a bit too much for her. I enjoy being in with her and seeing her, but I like to… you know… get out and about.' Robbie said.

Charlie did know what he meant. He had been there before in his own marriage with Jo. She was ready for the big sleep, and Charlie had too much 'going out' still to do.

'But you said you wanted to get out of town and maybe buy a place in the country…' Charlie said playing devil's advocate.

'I do, but I always need to come into town, you know?' Charlie looked perplexed.

'Work, Char. And work for me, always signals trouble.'

Charlie knew that feeling as well.

The men finished up sweaty and exhausted. Charlie felt invigorated and ready for a sauna and swim, so they went back to the changing rooms.

As they walked in, Robbie surveyed the scene like he usually did.

The Apex predator, checking for any potential threats.

As he did, he noticed something that bothered him. He breathed a little deeper, but kept looking back towards the toilet area.

'What's up, pal?' Charlie said, looking over.

'Here, is that OK to you?' Robbie whispered, pointing over at a man using the sink.

'What?'

'Geezer there, shaving…'

'How do you mean?'

'Like, why has that prick got to shave in here? A nice gym? What's the point in that?' Robbie's voice was louder and he was now eyeballing the guy in the mirror, whose face was half-covered in white foam.

'I think he's allowed to in here, just not in the sau-'

'-I mean he may be allowed too, but do you think it's OK?' Robbie said speaking loudly now. 'Just calm down a bit…'

'You all right, mate?' the guy said turning around and looking directly at Robbie.

He was a tall man, slender, but physically fit. He had that runner's build. A strong all-round physique without being overly muscular. His head was bald and his face… if he got the chance to finish… clean shaven.

'Yeah, I'm all right. Just wondering why you got to do that in here?' Robbie replied, stepping forward, his broken English making him sound even more threatening.

'What on earth has it got to do with you, pal? Not against the rules, is it?' he said, not giving an inch.

'It fucking should be. Disgusting! You ain't got a house or somewhere you can do that? It's a public place, a shared space!' Robbie continued.

Charlie was surprised that within the maelstrom of Robbie's life, he was so adamant about standards of personal hygiene.

The other guy fancied his chances though.

'Listen mate, I don't know what your problem is, but fuck off, will you?' he said, turning back to finish his shave.

With that Robbie leapt like a bear towards the

man, grabbing him with both hands.

He thrust his head into the mirror, which smashed in the process.

Robbie picked him up once more and threw him against the urinals, which looked decidedly painful, as the man landed awkwardly.

'Robbie, leave it will ya?'

Charlie began to grab his and Robbie's gear, stuffing it into their respective bags. He anticipated needing to make a speedy exit.

The man was on the floor. There was blood now trickling along the white tiles towards the drain in the centre of the room.

'Robbie, leave it!' Charlie boomed.

'Don't fucking shave in the gym, you *animal!*' Robbie bellowed, before leaving the man in a crumpled heap.

'Best get on our toes now, eh Charlie?'

24

Tara lay in a deep and comfortable sleep.

She normally had an ear out for the door, for when Charlie would come bustling back in, or for the letterbox, in case there was any mail. These days it always seemed to come in the afternoon.

Otherwise, she would be waiting for the cat to inevitably get bored, push the bedroom door open with her head and come into the room.

Then she would survey the room, doing at least one lap, before leaping on the bed and sitting on Tara's abdomen.

Today though, Tara's heard none of those things as she was in a dreamworld; somewhere far away where her lover and her were safe. She didn't want to wake up and fought the fact that she was stirring back to reality.

She rolled tentatively on to her side. Her abdominal pain was not bad, so she spent a few moments there, adjusting her eyes to the mustard feature wall with the large black palm trees.

Tara couldn't decide whether she still liked it or not. Since the latter stages of pregnancy, she was far more into neutral colours, but she really didn't have the energy to pick a new design, let alone change it.

In her peripheral vision, she noticed a flash of light from her phone.

She picked it up in case it was Charlie or her mum, wanting to see how she was. It was neither person though, when she unlocked it she noticed a text from an unrecognised number.

Her heart began to race as she opened it and she longed to be back in the safety of sleep.

Wakey, wakey, sweetheart. A little gift for you by the front door x

Tara checked the number, wondering if it was one of Charlie's old work phones.

Nothing matched.

She got up, put her dressing gown on and slowly moved downstairs. The cat flashed past her and into the kitchen, causing her heart to beat out of her chest.

She went into the hallway and up to the front door which she opened tentatively.

By her feet, there was a gift box with a gold card placed on top addressed to 'T.'

Tears welled in Tara's eyes. She looked out of the window and then immediately took the box to the front room. She checked the kitchen and looked out into the garden, to ensure that she wasn't being watched or followed.

Tara opened the card and began to read:

Dearest Tara,

I cannot stop thinking about you.

I think about how life is a series of choices and how each choice we make can take our lives in different directions. Like, had I have rung you or texted you after that night, how might things be different?

If I hadn't have got implicated in the Amy Green case, how might my life look?

Would we have spent more time together? Would Charlie Stone even be a part of yours?

Yes, life is about choices and it's never too late to change a wrong one.

This afternoon, your boyfriend will come back into the house and will tell you about another problem he has been a part of.

When are things going to change? Will they ever? Will you and your baby be safe?

I write this looking out to sea, as the bright sunlight glistens on the waves.

Don't you deserve better?

All my heart,

Troy.

Tara took up the gift box and opened it.

Inside it was a velvet photo album, which documented Tara's time with Charlie. There were photos of their first date, when they went to Bruges on a romantic getaway. Pictures of them at concerts in London, at restaurants and cavorting in bars. Then the nature of the photos changed to Charlie on his own. Caught on

CCTV, driving in the car, standing on the Leas. There were photos of her too alone. In the house, getting the shopping, arriving at her mum's.

Although there was no direct message, the photos in their order told a story, a love that was now somehow lost.

Tara, hormonal and overwhelmed, burst into snotty tears again.

She felt in her heart that Charlie and her were right together. But her head told her that in a way, Troy could offer her the security that she craved. Her time with Charlie had been a whirlwind at the beginning of their relationship, and it was thrilling. Things had changed. Everything had changed. She felt different and although she loved Charlie, she wanted to feel safe and secure.

In Troy's peculiar, slightly stalker-y way, he was watching out for Tara. Making sure she was OK.

She heard the key in the front door and hid the box and letter in a cupboard by the sofa. She wiped her face and eyes, trying to look vaguely normal.

Charlie bustled into the house, dropping his gym bag in the hallway and heading towards the laptop in the dining room.

'Hi, Charlie,' she mustered.

'Oh, sorry hun. Hi,' he returned. 'Are you OK? You've been crying?' He went towards her.

'Yes, fine. Bloody hormones!' she said, getting up to meet him.

'Oh, gosh. I'm sorry, hun. I just need to send an email to the gym. You are not going to believe what happened this afternoon!'

Tara nodded and smiled, following her man into the kitchen.

25

It was Sunday morning and Charlie drove towards Leeds Services, Junction 8 on the M20.

He was driving a little too fast in the morning sunshine, but he was excited to see his daughter for the first time in three months.

The music was blaring to Stormzy and Ed Sheeran's recent track, one of Maddie's favourites, or at least it was when he had last seen her, and Charlie couldn't help but sing along.

The fifteen-minute journey seemed to take an age, but eventually he pulled into the services and checked for Jo's blue VW Polo.

It was not there, but he noticed her distinctly recognisable face inside a silver BMW. She was sitting in the passenger seat with her arms folded. Next to her was a new face, a man who Charlie had never seen before.

Charlie looked at the man, who was in a beanie hat and had a short ginger beard. He looked across and their eyes met. Charlie nodded, but the man looked away.

There was movement in the back of the car.

Then there was an open door, a mop of mousy brown hair and Maddie, like a puppy dog, bounded out. He turned the engine of the car off and got out. Maddie ran towards him and they hugged. Charlie felt a pure, deep joy flood through him. A welcome relief from the trials his body had been put through recently.

'Pick up at 5.30pm.' Jo said flatly out of the window, before the BMW pulled away aggressively.

'Hi, dad!'

'Hi, sweet. Ready to go?'

'Yeah, of course.'

'Fancy a hot chocolate for the journey?'

Maddie looked at her father and smiled. She looked different. Her face seemed a little older and she was definitely taller. She wore a bright green beanie and a turquoise hoodie with black leggings.

She looked like she was sixteen years old to Charlie. She also looked like she could be an 'Anonymous' Hacker, or an extra from the Watch Dogs franchise. Not that he cared what she was wearing, he was just elated to see her. He put his arm around her neck and led her towards the coffee shop.

After a Frostino and a Black Americano, Charlie drove back to the house where Tara had made some brunch, consisting of French Toast with honey and chopped up apple pieces.

Maddie spent an hour or so getting reacquainted with the house and her bedroom, while Charlie and Tara sat in the front room together.

Charlie checked his phone while Tara turned the TV on. He had one message, from Trev,

Ready to go when you are. Finding out some strange things.

Charlie replied, *tomorrow mate, can come to yours whenever you like.*

Trev messaged back immediately, *the sooner the better. See you then.*

'Oh, goodness me…' Tara said into the ether.

'What's that, hun?' Charlie looked up at the TV screen and saw the bright yellow banner along the bottom that described 'Breaking News.'

'This virus, Charlie. It's getting worse. They are talking about closing shops and restaurants, stopping people seeing friends and family…'

Charlie thought about the M20 when it was gridlocked the other day.

'It's not good-'

'-What about the hospitals, Charlie? What about the baby?' Tara said, panic rising in her voice.

'It will be OK,' Charlie said, in that patronising way that only men can do, when discussing something of which they know nothing about.

Tara shot him a withering glance and Charlie looked back at his phone. He had nothing more to offer.

'Charlie, they are saying the hospitals are going to be filled with virus patients! There are going to be no beds. The NHS can't cope. There are no homebirths allowed anymore as they can't risk the ambulances…what if the baby gets the virus? What are we going to do?'

'It will be OK, sweet. By the time we give birth, we will be past the worst of it-'

'Well, that's not what they are saying on the

news!'

'You can't always believe the news, T. The mainstream media has its own agenda! How many times have we discussed, the need for a story... they're selling-'

'-Fear, Charlie. Yes, you have told me many times. Well, it's working. I'm bloody terrified.'

'Hi guys,' Maddie said, poking her head tentatively around the living room door.

'Shall we go into town?' Charlie said.

Tara didn't reply, but started to get slowly out of her seat.

The three of them got their coats and trainers on, before taking a slow walk into Ashford. It was a relaxed day and Charlie had booked bowling for the two of them, Tara said she wasn't allowed.

Maddie had the bumpers up and Charlie went rogue. After two games, they had won three stickers from the bowling staff and both Maddie and Charlie were able to get their names on the leaderboard, much to Charlie's joy. *I must find a new outlet for my competitiveness*, he thought to himself as he changed up a tenner for the arcade games.

First, they went on the basketball one, where you have to get as many hoops as possible in a certain time.

Maddie soon got bored when she realised it was harder than it looked, and moved on to the dancing game. As much as she tried to convince her dad to get on too, he refused, citing 'inappropriate footwear' as the reason, but Maddie knew that he was just too old and boring to have a go.

'So, on the way back do you fancy an ice cream?' Charlie asked.

Maddie's eyes grew large in excitement and she looked to Tara, who had a big, broad grin.

'While I am the size of a beached whale, I am going to eat whatever I want. So, I'm in.' Tara said with a smile.

Why not, Charlie smiled. It must be liberating, if only for a matter of months, you didn't have to worry about your weight!

As they got to the ice cream parlour, there was a queue of four people waiting out the front.

'What's this all about?' he said to Tara. 'There's empty tables in there.'

'Virus restrictions, hun. Only half the people allowed into these places now.' Tara returned, placing a hand on her belly. 'Oof! Mad, do you want to feel him kick?'

Maddie put her hand on Tara's belly.

'You feel him?' Tara asked.

She concentrated.

'No… not really…' Charlie and Tara both laughed, admiring her honesty.

It took a while to get seated, but eventually they were given a large booth in a corner. The pink leather of the seats contrasted with the black table which was wiped down vigorously before they sat down.

'This is the new thing, cleaning and washing everything down, you see, after every use…' Tara explained about the importance of cleanliness now that Great Britain was in the clutches of this new supervirus.

'Soon, we will be wearing masks everywhere we go…' she continued.

Charlie stared out of the window. He saw three men sitting on the park bench drinking some form of cheap, nasty spirit.

A woman came up, she looked dishevelled, potentially homeless, and started berating one of the men. He smiled at her, revealing a set of gnashers which were half missing, and looked like they hadn't been cleaned in a good few years.

She carried on shouting and the men continued to laugh. He took a big swig of his bottle and passed it on to his friend.

I hope you're OK up there Dave, Charlie thought to himself.

Dad, Dave, Jo and Polly. All this loss, all this defeat. Charlie felt a twinge of guilt twist inside of him, like an electric shock that hit him in the chest and spread through his upper body.

Why always me? What's wrong with me? Why do I always lose everyone I care about?

Charlie felt overwhelmed with sadness, with grief, with loss.

'Dad? Are you OK?' Maddie was pulling at his arm. 'Your breathing funny…'

Charlie came back to the room and noticed the two of them were looking at him. Tara looked concerned, while Maddie seemed to just find her dad's funny turn a little amusing.

'Oh, sorry…' Charlie took a moment to compose himself. 'Have you decided what you want guys?' Charlie said, wiping the sweat from his brow.

'Yes, dad. But have you?' Maddie said, as the waitress appeared at the table.

'Erm, yes...' He said.

They ordered and the waitress took the menus away.

Tara looked at Charlie.

'What's the matter? Are you feeling OK?' she asked, putting her hand on his leg.

Charlie was caught between bravado and authenticity.

'Yeah, fine. I just was watching those homeless guys over there. Thinking life must be pretty simple for them. Nothing really to worry about, except where the next drink comes from, eh?' Charlie chuckled nervously.

Tara looked at him incredulously and slowly took her hand from his leg.

They finished their desserts, paid, then took a slow walk back towards Willesborough.

There was about an hour before Maddie had to return to Jo, so Charlie and her sat down to do some drawing. They got the big pad of A3 out and Maddie turned on her iPad to find an exotic animal to copy.

Charlie doodled, unsure of what he wanted to create, but enjoying the opportunity to just sit with his daughter, chat inanely and not think too deeply about anything.

Half an hour passed as if it were five minutes and Maddie was left with a picture of a giraffe from the neck upwards, wearing a pair of dark sunglasses.

Charlie's picture was slightly different. There was a man sitting on a cloud meditating, while another man with long hair and a bottle in his hand fell into a pit of wolves and snakes.

Maddie analysed it.

'Bit weird dad, bit abstract, but good!' she said optimistically.

Charlie felt a little peculiar about it, so as Maddie went to get her bag ready for home, he screwed it up and placed it in the bin.

Maddie controlled, 'dad's jukebox,' all the way home. She chose one song, then dad did and so on.

The usual feeling of sadness was replaced with one of hope and renewed optimism.

Some binds he thought, *were maybe too strong to be broken, no matter how much people tried.*

Charlie was adamant that Jo had the power to destroy his relationship with Maddie. Jo believed that at the time of their separation in 2014, he would drift out of her life as so many dads tended to do. Terrified by the mother, of the system that works for them. Charlie kept his cool and years later, he was still here. An integral part of Maddie's life. This was something he was proud of, as was rebuilding his life with Tara and his unborn baby. He just couldn't understand why this sense of dread controlled him. Why everything could be going so well, and then the darkness would descend and none of it would matter to him.

'Hey dad, I had an awesome day. Let's not leave it so long, next time, yeah?' Maddie said, leaning over the gearstick to give her father a cuddle.

'Sure thing. I'm here anytime. I'll work out a plan with your mum moving forward,'

'Yeah!' she said, getting out of the car and running over to Jo, who stood outside the silver BMW, arms folded.

As Charlie reversed the car from the services, the phone rang with an unknown number.

It was already connected to the Bluetooth system, so Charlie pushed the button on the steering wheel to answer.

'Hello?'

'Charlie, it's Darren Jackson.'

'Oh hi, Skip.'

'How's it going?'

'Yeah, so-so. Ran into a bit of trouble with the Wolfire lot, but apart from that, things are OK.'

'Yeah, I heard. Sorry to hear about it. Wadham was released on a technicality, and he is running the Inland Border Facility now.'

'A technicality, eh? Something to do with Troy Wood, I daresay?' Charlie asked.

'Probably. Not worth digging into. The outcome is he is out and staying out, for now.'

'Yes, I gathered. You heard about his new friend? Got me good.'

'Yes, I did and that's kinda why I'm calling.'

'Oh really? Remember I am not a copper anymore, Darren. You don't have to try and help me.'

'It's not about the badge anymore. You were right, Charlie. There is something wicked about these people and I want to help you bring them down.' Jackson said firmly.

'Well, you have changed your tune, boss.'

'Listen, Charlie. Don't give me shit, all right? I'm trying to make amends for having to pull the poxy case in the first place.'

Charlie was pleased to hear his friendly voice. In the abyss he called his life, friends had been torn away brutally in recent times. He wanted a friend. He needed one.

'The thing is, Jacko… how do I know I can trust you? I mean, if Wolfire were putting it on you to get to me, this would be a-'

'-Charlie, give me more credit than that, please! I have been your friend; I am trying to help you!'

'How do I know that though, for sure?'

There was a pause and a deep breath on the other end of the line.

'I have had a dig around and Wolfire and

Thraxin are in cahoots. Wolfire control and release the virus… Thraxin provide the cure… they both make shit loads of money. It's a perfect storm.'

'Oh, really?'

'Yep, I'm gonna send you some files. That will help you join the dots… that facility is where they are working on the cure. Get this though, once they have it, they plan to release a new stronger strain… and only the elite get the cure, the poor are priced out of the market.'

'Jesus… so that's why those people are there? It's not immigration-'

'-Is it heck! They're guinea pigs for all sorts of 'off the record' stuff… shit got to go, Charlie…' the line went dead.

Charlie had another call coming in and accepted it.

In the background there was loud dance music, but no-one spoke.

'Hello?'

'CHARLIE, ME OLE SON!!!!'

'Hey, Rob, where are you?'

'Where do you reckon, pal?'

'Junction 13?'

'Bingo!'

'You're at the bingo?'

'You are a funny fucker… get yourself down here, mate!'

'Oh no, I shouldn't, we have work to do tomorrow. Getting back into that… you know where…'

Charlie didn't want to say the name on the line as he didn't know who was listening in.

'Yeah, course and I am with you for that, no problem. But you hear this country is about to go into lockdown. Right? Your mate Troy Wood's poxy virus is going to shut it all down for months. This could be our last chance to party for a while!' Robbie added.

Charlie checked his watch. It was coming up for 6pm.

'Yeah, go on, I'll come down for a bit.'

'Good lad, meet me at the Junction!'

'Sweet, ten minutes.'

26

Tara was at home in the bath.

This was the time of the day she really relished now, when it was coming to its end.

She, like most pregnant women, knew that it would be tough, but she hadn't imagined how tough.

The whole of the outer wall of her stomach hurt to touch. The weight of the baby was a dull ache in her abdomen. Her breasts seemed to have doubled in size, but much to Charlie's disappointment, were now no-go areas.

She had lit a candle, grabbed herself a cold can of diet coke and lay in the bath, scrolling her phone.

Tara was yet to tell anyone of her recent experiences with Troy. I mean, she felt hugely violated, and what Troy said to her confused her briefly, but her heart was with Charlie. She loved him for all his problems and all his flaws, she loved him and that was that, as far as she was concerned.

If Troy wanted to send super-drones to the house to spy on her, good luck to him.

She felt large and unattractive, so he could knock himself out for all she cared.

Yes, life could be a lot better, but it could be a lot worse.

She was having a baby. Charlie loved her in his… unique way. He was going to catch the baddies. It would all be OK.

When she got out of the bath, she would get her dressing gown and make them both a tasty dinner, maybe even put a couple of beers in the fridge for him, he should be back any minute.

Just a few more minutes in the bath first though…

Her phone buzzed.

Hi hun. Just gone for a few drinks. Won't be too long though. Have dinner and I'll see you a little later. X x x

'Bloody hell!' she said out loud, before immersing her head and shoulders under the bath water.

Junction 13 was filled with its regular clientele. Mr. Magoo was standing at the bar looking miserable, forlorn. Sharn swept the floor and smiled sweetly as Charlie bustled in. Robbie was in the corner playing on his phone and Jeff was talking to two guys near the bar who Charlie did not recognise.

'All right, son?'

'Yeah, good,' Charlie sat down and noticed his favourite beer was waiting for him where he sat.

He smiled up at Robbie, who nodded back at him.

'So, this is the last hurrah.' Robbie said, he seemed pretty sad.

'What do you mean?'

'Fucking lockdown! Starting tomorrow,' Robbie continued, nodding to the screen that usually showed sport, but was airing a special news bulletin.

'It won't be forever, Rob.'

'It will feel like it, all cooped up, fenced in. Not able to go out, see anyone…'

'Jeez, that happened quickly,' Charlie said, taking a sip of his pint. 'I thought you wouldn't mind it. A few weeks quiet time in with Becky?'

'Fuck her, mate. We're over!' Robbie said a little too loudly.

'Oh, really?'

'I reckon so mate. Anyway, Trev's going to come down in a bit and we can sort out tomorrow.' Robbie said.

'Righto.'

The men waited in silence before Trev appeared, sketchily nodding at Sharn who waited patiently for a drink order from him that never arrived.

'How's it going?' he greeted them.

'Yeah, good mate. Fancy a drink?' Charlie offered.

'You're kidding. I can't drink their stuff. You don't know what's in it.'

'Go on Trev. What do you mean?' Robbie said smirking to Charlie.

'Government chemicals, addling your brain, making you all docile and sedated…'

'Isn't that just the alcohol?' Charlie asked.

'No, *smartarse!* Anyway, about tomorrow. Let's get sorted.' Trev said, pulling out a phone and a small hand-held device that fired up with video footage of the Border Facility. 'Our goal is to get enough evidence to bring down Paul Wadham. Charlie, this is the second time you have been here, so you should be doubly motivated. We want to get through their high security system, and into Wadham's office and extract what we can find. We already have enough with the emails from Thraxin to suggest some form of foul play. We just want to build the case, so there is no chance of this serpent ever being released again.'

'Well, he got out once-'

'Exactly, Charlie. And we need to make sure that we put him away for good this time.'

Trev appeared convincing, but something about Wadham's release made Charlie feel uneasy. If Wadham got out once, what's to say he couldn't do it again? The system was geared so that the powerful and elite could manipulate it, which is one of the main reasons why Charlie felt he needed to be away from the Force.

Trev pulled up live CCTV images from the facility.

'How are you getting these pictures, Trev?' Charlie asked.

'I hacked the internal security system and have briefly taken control of their 'mothership.' My surveillance suggests that on Sunday afternoon, in particular, they are a wee bit lax in their operations. The guard on duty is a football fan and tends to be watching whatever game is on Sky, via his phone.'

'Nice.'

'What I can do is replace the live images with scrolling images that were recorded earlier, so you can sneak in undetected.'

Robbie and Charlie nodded.

'Still, let's be quick, eh? If he does notice us in the system, it will be a major problem. Right, if I zoom in here, can you see this manhole cover in the far corner of the courtyard?'

The men looked intently.

'Right, so there is an entry point to the sewer about forty metres to the west of the facility, which I suggest is your only viable way to get in. We open the manhole that's around fifty metres from the Facility and you come up through there. Your problem is that when you come out, it is difficult to know who will be on guard and where, but if we hit them early tomorrow am, there are usually just two security lads.'

'Wait, what about Frank?' Charlie said eagerly.

'Let's not alert anyone to what we are doing-'

'-But he's a mate. A good mate of yours. You can ask him, he'll be golden-'

'-No mate, lets not get him involved. The other issue is when you head down into the sewer, initially, there is a guard point that is supposedly keeping watch over 'potential threats' which, of course, you are. What we really need is a distraction…'

'Well, where will you be, Trev?' Charlie asked.

'Good question, I could be the distraction, but if I am, then I am not watching you now, am I?'

Charlie pondered who he could trust to be a diversion. In the past he had good people, friends, like Polly and Dave. Now there was no-one.

'Well, let's come back to that. Once you are in, Charlie, there are documents that you need to obtain from a computer in Wadham's office which is going to be incredibly well guarded and secure.'

'Well, we love a challenge, don't we!' Robbie smirked.

'I would suggest on site, in total, there will be ten guards, possibly six, but worst case, ten. Now, two of them will be in the courtyard, two will be on guard point, hopefully dealing with whatever distraction we can find, two will be on reception and won't be an issue for you. The others, probably through the mystery black door and towards Wadham's office.'

'What about the tools, Trev?'

'Don't worry, you will be sorted, thanks to my personal collection.' Trev said. The men looked at each other and Charlie took a big slug of his drink.

'Any questions?' Trev asked, as the men digested the information.

'What exactly am I looking for?' Charlie asked.

'You my friend, will be furnished with a USB, and what I want you to do is a file dump from Wadham's computer onto it.'

'Right...'

'Sounds complicated, but trust me, it will be easy. I'll run you through it in the car and I will also be in your earpiece... co-ordinating...'

'Co-ordinating?'

'Yes, Charlie. Is that OK? Or do you want us all to go in blind and have no communication or intel?'

'No need to be defensive, Trev. Just making sure we are clear.'

'Any intel Charlie, I will get it immediately and quite frankly, it's horses for courses. The people should be on the ground, are... and I can keep you as safe as I can from afar.'

'Fair enough.' Charlie thought about this. Again, paranoia and distrust rose in him like a wave. *How well did he know this Trev? Could he really trust him? What about Robbie? How do we know they're not...* the darkness went to grip him, but Charlie was shaken from his oncoming nightmare by the sound of the door to Junction 13 being flung open.

In stormed the petite yet ferocious frame of Becky, Robbie's on-off other half.

'You fucking bastard, I can't fucking believe you!' she yelled towards her boyfriend.

'Calm down for fuck's sake!'

'No, you fucking calm down!' she shrieked, aiming a blow at his head as he rose from his chair.

'Leave it out, Becky!' he said.

'You think you can do what you bloody well like, coming in and out, doing powder in my house, and now this!'

'W-what?' Robbie said, timidly.

'You know what! You have been seeing that woman, haven't you?'

'Who, Tilly?'

'Who the fuck is Tilly, you prick? I meant your fat ex, Laura!' she boomed.

'Oh, yeah… Laura… I haven't seen her babe, I promise…'

'Fuck you, dickhead. She text me, sent me screenshots, of you two together!'

Just as Becky went to launch herself at their table, Charlie moved into the way, scooping her up and taking her outside. As he held her squirming body, he looked back at Trev who nodded at him sagely.

It looked like they had found their 'distraction.'

27

After Becky's episode, Charlie didn't really feel like staying out, and anyway, he needed to get some rest.

He had manoeuvred Becky outside, calmed her and assured himself that she was safe to carry on with her day.

Obviously, the rage in her mind was justified, but what she really wanted was to make things right, and get the attention of her on/off lover, who was very much feeling 'off' given her recent outburst.

After dealing with her, Charlie drove back to Ashford.

He entered the house at just after 8pm, and Tara was sitting on the sofa watching the Tv programme, Friends.

'Hey,' he called through.

'Hey, dinners on the stove.'

Charlie took a small bowl from the cupboard and spooned some Bolognese in.

He sat down with Tara.

'Been out?' she asked, not averting her eyes from the screen.

'Yeah, just for one. I always feel a bit blue when Maddie goes.' he said, between mouthfuls.

'Fair enough,' she returned monotone.

'Tomorrow morning, I will be gone when you wake up. Got a real lead in the Wood case-'

Tara snorted with derision.

'What?'

'Nothing. Just, nothing.' she said. She knew how important resolving the case was for him.

Even if she explained how she felt, even if she discussed about how she felt scared and tired and lonely, that even if she was terrified and she was about to have a baby and she missed the times when they could go out and talk, really talk… even if she said that despite her state and everything else, that she was being pursued by Charlie's arch nemesis… what would it matter?

Charlie had a case to solve.

'You know I-'

'-I know, Charlie. I know. I'm off to bed. You coming?' Tara said, slowly raising herself from the sofa. He finished his pasta and followed.

The alarm buzzed Charlie awake at 4.15am.

It was dark outside and he slid himself out of bed and towards the bathroom, careful to not wake his fiancée.

He had a quick shower, first half warm, second half ice cold, to wake him up, before putting on a pair of combat trousers and a black sweater.

He picked up his phone and wallet and slid his black boots on too.

By the time he had quietly shut the front door, Trev's Land Rover gently pulled up at the kerbside.

Charlie had butterflies as he jumped in the back

of the vehicle. He looked up at the dark bedroom window, almost certain he could see someone's eyes peering through the slats in the blinds.

'Morning, Charlie,' Trev said from the front of the vehicle.

'Hello,' Charlie spoke, surveying the car. Robbie was in the front, Trev was driving and Charlie sat in the back alongside Becky.

He shot her a smile, as she gazed mindlessly out the back window.

'Don't you start,' she said, with a fiery glance at Charlie.

'What?'

'You're lucky I'm here, so keep yourself to yourself, all right?' she barked in Charlie's direction.

'Easy now, you two,' Trev chuckled from the front seat.

'How you doing, Charlie?' he asked.

'Good. I was wondering though, what about uniforms? That may make life easier in there...'

'Clever boy. Check under the seat, two fresh and unworn Wolfire security outfits. It's a tight knit operation in there, so if you get spotted they will be likely to sniff you out as imposters. The outfits may buy you a few minutes though, if you think fast.'

'Hm.' Charlie eyed the kit before taking the smaller one and began to disrobe. He wondered how Trev had got hold of these, but thought it best not to ask.

He glanced at Becky, given that he was about to take off his trousers.

She gave him a wry smile, 'Oh, please.'

Feeling suitably derided, he continued.

Trev took the Land Rover through Wye, so they could come into the facility via the backroads, under the cover of darkness.

The facility area loomed large ahead of them, as they headed into the valley. Trev pulled the vehicle to a halt.

'Right, out.' he said.

He came around to the back of the truck and opened it, Charlie jumped out.

'Bex, stay there for a moment please,' Trev said softly.

'OK, the manhole is about four metres south-east of here, in fact you can see it over there. Once we've opened it, you will need about four minutes to make your way through it and to the exit point. You need to stay directly south and follow the path. There will be other routes, but this is the one you need. It is forty-two metres to the manhole cover you want, so keep a rough count, although there should be no other exit points around it.'

Charlie nodded, as Trev pulled two guns from the bag, one shotgun and one pistol.

'Take these, it would be prudent not to use them, but just in case.'

'What's your plan for the diversion?' Charlie

asked, placing the gun in his side pocket.

'Well, glad you asked! Just up the lane to the left there, a two-minute walk, I have stowed an old, Ford Fiesta. Bex is going to get into it and drive to the gate and make a bit of a scene. By that time, I will be on the brow of the hill, just thirty metres due west of this location, where I will be monitoring the operation.'

'Erm, not being funny. How can you do that when there are massive walls around the gaff?' Robbie said, his big face screwed up, his brow furrowed.

Trev shook his handheld device at him.

'Ah, the wonders of modern technology,' Charlie confirmed.

'Yes, I can hack the CCTV and probably keep a better eye on you than if I was there. Any major problem, one shot from this bad boy and those Wolfire guards will come running.' Trev tapped his sniper rifle.

'Anything else?' Trev asked.

There was collective silence.

'All right then, good luck.'

****

Tara woke with a jolt.

It was 5.15am and darkness filled the room. There was a cold, empty space next to her where Charlie should have been.

She came to and heard the deep vibration of her

phone against the hard floor, buzzing to life.

'Hello?' she croaked.

'Hi, Tara? Sorry, it's Darren Jackson. Is Charlie there? His phone's off, I can't get hold of him.'

'No, he's uh… well, he's not here…'

'Tara, do you know where he is?'

'I don't…no …'

'Listen, it's really important I know where he is, he could be in danger…'

'Wh- why? What do you mean, Jacko?'

'If I can get to him, he'll be fine, but, *where is he?*'

'I don't know! He said he had an operation he was involved in. Something to do with what happened to him last week. He doesn't give me any details after that whole thing with Jennifer Green.'

'Right, OK, that helps. Listen don't worry. I will sort everything. You relax, OK?'

The phone line went dead.

Yeah, great. I'll just… relax. Tara rolled over into the middle of the bed and anxiously hugged her belly.

****

'It fucking stinks down here!' Robbie said, holding his nose and narrowly avoiding a chute of brown water from hitting him in the back. 'Jesus!'

'Stay focused, buddy. It wont take long down here.'

Charlie was counting the metres but also had an eye on the time, they had fifty-four seconds before Becky was having her Oscar moment, so the men were under pressure.

Charlie led the way, shuffling forward on the metal sewer bridge that led under the Border Facility.

After a while, Charlie became oblivious to the foul smell and zoned out to the sound of the running water that seemed to be ever-present.

In the darkness he could hear rats but not see them, so focusing on moving forward was his only priority.

'Just up ahead, I think…'

'Thank fuck for that,' Robbie mused.

****

Becky got behind the wheel of the Ford Fiesta that Trev had left near the Facility. She opened the sun visor to reveal the key, placed it in the ignition and took a deep breath.

She knew how much trouble she could get into; she knew how risky this was, how dangerous these people were. But she had always wanted to be a policewoman, despite her dodgy upbringing. She knew her dad, who was a small-time dealer, would never have allowed that, so she suppressed the urge. Although she was about to create a massive scene, she knew she was doing something for the greater good. To catch this bastard, Paul Wadham, who killed those girls on Sunny Sands.

She put her foot on the accelerator and screamed towards the large, black gates of the Border Facility.

****

'OK, hold the clip, while I prise the cover open,' Charlie said, brown liquid dripping onto his face. The sewer had a warm, filthy stench to it, grime on every surface.

'Right, here goes…' Charlie prised with his knife at the cover, careful not to attract any Wolfire guards.

On the other side of the manhole, Frank was leaning against the wall in the courtyard, puffing on a cigarette, looking up at the night sky.

****

Frank thought wistfully about his recent holidays; Crete, Majorca, Marrakesh… one bonus of this messed up job was that it did pay rather well.

He wondered when he and his girlfriend, Judith, would next be able to jet off to the heat.

Some reports say this lockdown could be over six months long, with things not back to 'normal' for two years. *Two years!*

He would sneak out of the country on a dinghy

rather than wait that long to get the sun on his back again. Of course, he had the English summers, but they weren't the same.
He checked his phone:

Hi F-dog. Dinner is in the oven for you. Wake me up if you want when you get back x x x x

Frank sniggered to himself. F-dog. She was funny. He had bagged himself a good one there.

Thanks, love you Judy-poo x x x

he sent back before he heard a creaking sound, like metal clanking or twisting.
'What in the hell is that?' he said to himself.
The gaffer told the boys to be extra vigilant, there were warnings of an imminent attack on the facility.
Frank cocked his 9mm pistol and crouched, like he was told to do in his training.
The clunking of metal again. It seemed to be coming from the other side of the courtyard. Frank cautiously took small steps towards the sounds.
A loud crunch of metal upon metal followed, a crash, glass shattering and then loud voices and the alarm. Red light flashed, flooding the courtyard in an orange glow.
Frank's radio crackled into life.
'All personnel to the reception area!'   Frank

immediately ran towards the commotion.
****

Becky knew not to wear her seatbelt and to dive out of the car just before impact. She wasn't stupid.

It was after that she needed to remember what Trev had told her.

Having performed her stunt she got up, wiping the dust from her clothes and saw two guards that quickly became three, and then four, pointing guns at her from the towers.

'Put your hands up!' One of the Wolfire soldiers shouted.

'I just want to see my boyfriend! You got him in here! I know you have!' Becky screeched, in her most convincing estuary anguish.

'Hands up!'

'I'll put my hands up when you take me to see him!'

'Miss, put your hands up!'

'Take me to see him!' She kept her arms firmly by her sides. A steely grit and determination took hold. She was stronger than these men with their guns. She had more minerals, more about her.

She waited it out, like a gunfight in a Western, minus the tumble weed.

The conviction in Becky's voice forced the soldiers to lower their guns.

'Right, let her in!'

****

The cover finally caught and Charlie could manoeuvre it to the side. The cold night air hit them, an awesome relief from the stench of the sewer.

'Right, give me a bunk up,' Charlie said lifting his foot.

He raised himself up and poked his head through the manhole cover, anxious that one sighting of him, one bullet, and it would all be over.

Luckily, the commotion and the alarm meant that the courtyard was deserted.

Charlie did a complete 360 to ensure he wasn't sighted, and when he was comfortable, he drove himself up and onto the hard concrete of the courtyard.

He stayed with one knee on the ground and put his hand to his side, checking his pistol was there.

He waited for Robbie, offering him a hand up as he struggled through the tight metal frame.

'Fuck me, that's a bit snug,' he whispered.

Charlie put his finger to his mouth, to indicate quiet and then nodded to a far wall, away from the roving eye of the CCTV.

Charlie was aware that Trevor should have dealt with that, but better to be safe than sorry.

The courtyard was empty and silent. Their

breath left them as clouds and were the only thing moving in the stillness of the night.

Charlie took out his mobile phone and pulled up the plan of the Facility. He could see that it was set into blocks, four of them, A-D. They each had their letter above the door leading from the courtyard.

There was also the fifth block, black door, no letter.

The alarm stopped and the men looked at one another. This meant that the guards had got whatever situation Becky had caused under control and would be heading back to their positions soon.

Charlie motioned to Robbie to follow him. He stayed low and moved silently towards the C-Block, as it was the nearest door to them.

Like all of them, it was protected by an electronic card reader. Trevor had already furnished the men with two fake identity cards in their uniform packs.

He said there was a fairly large chance of them not working on the readers, but would come in handy even if they couldn't open the doors.

Charlie moved towards the door and swiped his card across the reader which flashed red. Robbie tried his, the same outcome.

Charlie looked through the door, into the block, and saw no movement. He stood against the wall and took a deep breath, contemplating his next move.

As he did, he heard a large thud as Robbie's size twelve opened the door emphatically.

Charlie couldn't believe what he had witnessed.

'Don't start…' Robbie said, raising his gun and making his way through the door.

Charlie fought against saying anything, since no-one seemed to be alerted.

They were in a bright, sterile corridor, filled with rooms that were in effect small prison cells, just like the one Charlie was incarcerated in.

They moved through the building slowly. The rooms were filled with male prisoners, all of them were dark or tan-skinned and appeared as if they were from the middle east or Asia.

'Are we busting these lot out or what?' Robbie whispered.

'Hundred percent, if we can,' Charlie returned. 'Let's keep going for now.'

The men were all beaten and battered. Most were lying on the empty floors, lost somewhere between life and death.

Charlie looked through the final door and saw a man convulsing, with the thousand-yard stare, naked.

What had they done to deserve such a fate?

'Let's finish the operation and come back for these guys.'

Charlie felt a bead of cold sweat run down his neck and along his spine. He dreaded to think what their fate would be if they didn't free them. Robbie stopped in his tracks, then moved backwards out of sight as the corridor of the C-Block took a sharp turn to the right.

He intimated that there were guards coming this way as Charlie could hear chatting and laughing in the distance.

There was nowhere to hide, except back towards the courtyard and even then, they were out in the open, sitting ducks.

Charlie looked at Robbie and pushed his back from the wall.

'All right lads,' Charlie said, nodding at the men as they came around the corner.

'I haven't seen you here before?' One of the guards said to Charlie.

'Oh yeah, new today,' Charlie said, holding up his badge, which was perused in detail.

Trevor had done well; it was precisely the same as the badge his opposite number was wearing, with a different name and picture.

'OK. I'll just go and check this out with the boss,' the other lad said.

Charlie signalled to his partner, before grabbing the first guy and placing him in a chokehold.

As he fell to the floor, Robbie tiptoed up behind the second guy and smashed his temple with the butt of his gun.

'What we gonna do with these melts?' Robbie continued.

Good question. Charlie wasn't sure. He looked back down the corridor, noticing the CCTV camera move rapidly from them to the left, and at a ninety-degree angle. It was pointing at an office space at the far end of the corridor, near the courtyard.

'Nice one, Trev,' Charlie nodded at the camera and signalled for Robbie to drag the other body up the corridor and into the small office.

Once the bodies were safely in, they left, shutting the door behind them.

They went back through the corridor and Charlie consulted his plan again. He needed to find anything that proved that this was illegal, unlawful and morally corrupt.

He moved through the block and noticed the sign above him read B- Block.

It had the same set up, bright and clinical, and at least a dozen cells. Charlie looked through the windows and this time noticed a number of women… older women, again of varying ethnic origins.

Charlie intimated to Robbie to check the other side of the corridor.

'Yep, all old girl's mate,' he whispered.

'Weird,' Charlie returned, before taking a few photos with his phone as evidence of what was going on here.

Jacko must have been right. This was no way a genuine Border Facility. Why were these people being separated and held in different groups?

The men moved around towards the next block, which was 'A.'

They could see that there was a guard in the

distance, so again hung back whilst they decided what their next move would be.

28

'Here, Arnold. What the hell do you think we should do with her?' Frankie said, staring at the screen in front of him.

He watched the woman run at the door and waited for the metal crunch of skin and bone.

She had stopped screaming though, which was merciful.

'Arnold?'

'Fucking leave her in there until she tires herself out. Then go and have a bit of fun with her, I reckon,' Arnold said, joining his underling at the screen.

'Very funny,' Frank said.

Arnold looked up at him and their eyes met.

'Listen, Frankie, it isn't everyday a present like this tart, drops in old Arnie's lap. She's a tidy little bird. I'm having a go on her.'

'Jesus Christ, Arnie. That isn't funny.' Frank said, deciding it best to go out for a long cigarette break.

The sound in the cell had quietened and Arnold leered at the screen. The blonde woman, who ten minutes ago was screaming out the front for her boyfriend, had finally tired herself out.

Arnold smiled, 'that's my cue.'

****

Charlie and Robbie watched as Frank made his

way out of the office of the A Block and into the courtyard.

They could hear talking, but not what was being said, so they knew there was another man in the office. Now was the time to strike.

They made their way down to the office, checking the cells as they went. All women again, this time younger, from the ages of roughly eighteen to forty, all grouped together.

Charlie took some cursory snaps of the cells, before heading to the empty office with Robbie behind him.

The men looked up at the screen and noticed that there was no sound.

The other guard was in one of the cells. It took Robbie a few moments to work out what was happening. Once he did, it was like a slow-motion video, Charlie was powerless to stop the events that were about to occur, he could only follow and fail to pacify his friend.

Robbie found the correct cell and burst through the door. He grabbed Arnold who was lying on top of Becky, and lifted him into the air.

Arnold's trousers were around his ankles and Charlie realised the unpleasantness of what was unfolding in front of him.

Robbie took Arnold by the neck and flung him like a cur across the room. His back snapped with a crack and Robbie was on him again, smashing and mashing.

Charlie knew it was futile to try and intervene.

Robbie's power was immense at the best of times, unstoppable at the worst.

Becky, who had recovered herself, had begun by trying to get at her attacker, Arnold, and was now pulling at Robbie, trying to prevent the inevitable from occurring.

Charlie pulled her away from danger and to the doorway, just as Robbie dealt his final blow.

The corner of the room was a blood-soaked mess. Charlie was unsure he had witnessed a scene quite like this in all of his years of service. It was like he had returned from a hypnosis, an out of body experience, and he could now see the reality of what had occurred.

As Robbie raised himself from Arnold's lifeless body, Frank came running into the cell.

'Fuck! Charlie? What are you doing here?' he uttered.

'You? You, you prick! You were going to let him *rape* her?' Robbie spat, moving towards his old colleague.

'How could you?' Charlie added.

'No. I, no…' Robbie reached for him, but his bloodlust had clearly been abated. He held him by the scruff of the neck, eyeballing him.

'Let's finish what we came here to find,' Charlie whispered.

'Yeah, I can help you. I can get you access to whatever it is you came here for. Whatever it is you need. This place is fucked up, mate. You don't want to be here any longer than you have to,' Frank continued.

Robbie was breathing heavily, eyes wide like an animal, snarling and foaming at the mouth.

He was unsure what to do with Frank. He understood that there was a hierarchy, yet he was appalled by cowardice. Frank sensed his conundrum.

'Listen, mate. I didn't know what he was going to do. I half thought he was pissing about, you know. I find him fucking disgusting, so I just... listen. The boss here trusts me, OK? He knew Arnie was on his way out, on borrowed time, they just needed a way to get rid of him.' Frank spluttered, trying to please his friend.

'Well, they don't need to worry now,' Becky said, pulling Robbie towards her, looking at the claret mess that was in the corner of the cell.

'Look, they even gave me higher level access, Paul wanted me to work directly for him, under him, said I had potential. Here take this.' Frank held out his card key, looking Robbie dead in the eye.

Robbie accepted it, without saying a word, still mulling over his options.

'Go, get what you need. I will clean this up, cover for you if anyone comes,' Frank said.

Robbie grunted, and Charlie was more than happy with that arrangement.

'Bex, you stay here with Frank. If you touch a hair on her head...' Robbie started, the rage rising inside him.

'It will be fine,' Charlie said, placing his hand on his friend's arm to pacify him.

'Right, lets finish the job.' Robbie said, leaving the cell and looking towards the black metal door, that was just visible across the courtyard.

29

The men checked their surroundings and they were alone. Charlie took the opportunity to phone Trev and check in.

'Well, so much for fucking get in - get out, quiet as a mouse!' Trev said down the phone.

'Oh, leave it out...' Robbie muttered, overhearing the conversation.

'It's happened now and it hasn't compromised us, *somehow*. Trev why is it so quiet, seems hardly guarded at all?' Charlie asked.

'It's the usual number of guards they normally have on. Four you have dealt with, my prediction is two behind the black door, while the others are on guard post and reception. Maximum of ten, but sometimes only six, remember?'

'Hm. OK, so behind the door... it's where we're headed now. We have access via Frank's key. Any advice?' Charlie continued.

'Fuck knows what's going on behind there. No CCTV, no fuck all. It's a black hole. *Careful.*'

'Right.'

'Get in, get out. Quick as you can.'

'Yep.'

The phone went dead and Charlie checked the courtyard once more before opening the electronic door with Frank's key.

There was a guard stationed on one of the posts in the north-east corner of the Facility. Charlie checked he was facing away, before motioning Robbie to scarper through the courtyard and across to the door.

They hit the other side of the wall and waited, checking for noises or any sign of activity from behind it.

It was silent. Only the cool, night breeze whistled past them.

'OK, let's go.' Charlie said.

Robbie nodded as Charlie took out the higher-level access key.

He placed it on the reader. There were whirring sounds, electronic bleeps and burps before the reader stated that the key needed to be swiped too.

Charlie followed the instructions nervously.

Again, there was a slight pause, an anxious wait as the card reader decided whether to permit them.

The guard moved from his spot in the north-east tower, along the far wall and into their eye line. He was still facing the opposite way, thankfully.

Eventually the card reader flashed green, the door clanked. A dead lock inside it opened.

There were sounds now and as Charlie gently pulled the door open; he was met with the desperate sounds of whimpering and moaning.

The men slipped inside, being sure to pull the door shut and lock it behind them.

It was dark, not pitch black, but their eyes would need time to adjust, so Charlie turned on the torch app that was part of his mobile phone. The beam was small but bright, which allowed them to get their bearings in the dark, dank corridor.

They were in a passage; it was brick built and tight. There was a warm, sweetness to the air. A scent Charlie knew, but couldn't place. Off-putting and strange in a facility such as this. Like freshly-baked bread in prison, it just wasn't right.

They shuffled through the first corridor and turned immediately right.

Charlie flashed the light into the darkness, and they were in another brick-built corridor, this time shorter, that led straight towards a sharp, ninety-degree angle left.

Again, they moved forward and Charlie poked his head around the corner as they reached the end of the corridor.

There was a new door and a new sign above it which was handwritten and read, 'The Pleasure Centre.'

The whimpers grew louder.

Charlie took a deep breath and pushed on to the new door, which was unlocked.

They stepped through and into a new, larger room. Charlie shone the beam around, trying to find a light switch.

There had to be electricity, why else was it so warm?

As Charlie flashed the light, he noticed human flesh in the corner of the long room. They slowly moved forward nearer to feminine sounds, whispering and quiet conversation. This turned to wailing and shouting.

'What the fuck?' Robbie said.

Charlie located a switch on the wall and flicked it, illuminating the room.

The mound of flesh became clear. There were around ten or so young girls, naked, cowering in the corner of the room, holding each other.

'It's OK! It's OK… we're here to help…' Charlie said.

There were two rooms to the side of the long room where the females were kept.

One had a deep, red glow from it and the other had an array of various sexual devices, and what appeared to be a medical table.

'Jesus…' Charlie said, moving towards the rooms to get a better understanding of what was happening here.

'What the fuck's going on here?' Robbie spoke into the air, to no-one in particular.

'You aint one of 'em, are ya?' one of the girl's spoke.

'One of who?'

'Them! The guards, *the men…*'

Robbie looked down at his uniform.

'What us? Fuck no.'

'We are here to help get you out…but… what is this?'

Charlie looked further into the rooms.

Metal surgical implements, bright lamps, red lights, what looked like a sex swing…. Charlie got the picture.

'They brought us here. Took me off the street when I runaway and then they keep us here – "The Pleasure Centre" they call it.'

Charlie shuddered, facing the girl who was speaking. He was lost for words.

'How old are you?' he asked, not really wanting to know the answer.

'Firteen.' The girl said.

Charlie looked around for a cover or a cloak, but it was pointless. There wasn't anything in the room. Just that sweet, sickly smell… that uncomfortable warmth.

The rest of the girls slowly started getting to their feet and moving towards them, behind the girl who was speaking.

'Lana's twelve. Esme is thirteen and Debbie is eleven.' The girl said pointing the others out.

'You're… English… this is a border…'

The girl laughed.

'Don't be stupid, mate. Most of us here are English. And this ain't no border facility.'

Charlie looked at the girl's dirty skin. He noticed some fresh wounds along with scars on her torso.

There was deep bruising around her privates and genitalia.

'I mouth off to the guards. To the big man. Means they are more likely to pick on me and leave the rest alone. Sometimes it don't work like that. Usually, it does.'

Charlie was bemused. One thing was for sure, if he could get the girls out, he wouldn't need his photographs for evidence anymore.

There was an office towards the back of the room. Locked of course.

'Here,' Charlie called out and began attempting to bust it open.

Robbie, white-faced, joined him and they forced it open.

There was a white desk in an otherwise empty room. The draws in the desk were locked.

'Keep an eye out, will you?' Charlie said to Robbie.

****

Frank sat Becky down in the office and made her a cup of tea.

She was calm and seemed to trust him. She had been put through the ringer tonight, but if some good comes of it, it would be worth it she thought to herself.

Frank checked regularly for any activity, but it was quiet. There would be no need for any guards to head onto his block, but he monitored the cameras anyway.

Frank started clearing the pile of goo and muck his old friend and boss, Arnold, had become. As he was picking bits of his brain and fragments of bone from out of the floor, Frank shed a tear for his old pal.

Despite his sadness, he was aware that he was lucky not to suffer the same fate. The old dog had a temper on him. Robbie's bite was far, far worse than his bark.

Frank required yet another roll of J-Cloth from under the kitchen sink, and at the same time he checked on Becky, who was staring into the distance, blowing her tea.

He left her to it and got back on his knees, when the door to the A Block burst upon and he was presented with the suited figure of Paul Wadham, surrounded by three heavily-armed personal guards.

'Hello Frank!' Paul called out as he turned the corner into the cell. 'Jesus fucking Christ, what on earth has happened here? Did you do this to him? What a bloody mess!'

'No, err… boss… it was, uh…' Frank was caught out. He didn't know what he could or should say.

'Come on Frank…. Talk to me… or I can check the CCTV…'

'Well… um…'

'Right, check the CCTV…' Wadham said to one of his cronies.

'There seems to be a problem with the system, sir. The CCTV is down…'

'What? Wells! You'd better start talking!'

'OK, boss. It was me…'

Wadham raised a pistol from his side and shot Frank twice in the chest and once in the head.

'Silly boy. I thought you were cleverer than that.' Wadham said, placing the gun back in his right-hand suit pocket.

'Right, well, he won't be much help now. Onwards, let's find these intruders.'

The men marched out, back through the courtyard and towards the black metal door.

****

Charlie jimmied the lock to the desk drawer and pulled the contents out onto the table.

There were papers which Charlie didn't fully understand, but pertained to the sale of products from an online furniture store.

The prices were surprising too… ten grand for a sofa…. seven for a 'Sofia' cushion. He followed Trev's precise instructions and was surprised at how easy he found it to copy the data from the computer onto the stick Trev had given him. After a couple of minutes he was done, he grabbed the stick, collected up the papers and came out of the office. Robbie was standing nervously with the girls, who sat and talked to one another as if he wasn't even there.

'I have what we need. Now, how are we going to get these girls out of here?' Charlie asked, scratching his head.

'We could take a punt and try and get them down through the sewers?' Robbie replied.

'Yes, yes, Robbie! We can get them out that way!

Good thinking.' Charlie said.

'What's going on, boss? You going to be the hero and get us out or what?' the gobby girl said.

'Yes, yes we are. I'm going to find some clothes or covers; the night out there is cold. We have friends in here who will help us. We will come back for you.' Charlie said, now frantic, stuffing as many of the documents he found in the office in his pockets and zipping them up.

The girl sneered at Charlie, he looked her dead in the eye.

'We will get you out of here.' He said, with a steely resolve that convinced her.

For the first time her guard dropped and she nodded at him. He reached out and touched her arm, comforting her.

She accepted the invite and put her arms around his neck. Initially, he felt uncomfortable, but he realised this girl was damaged, brutalised and used as meat. She just needed a moment of love.

'Be ready, we'll be a few minutes.'

There was elated chatter amongst the girls and for the first time since they could remember, hope. A brief crack of light.

Charlie and Robbie bustled out of the room and back towards the black door.

As they approached the door it unlocked, and in walked Wadham and his henchmen.

'Oh, fuck me. I should have known it was you! Wont you ever just *fuck off*?' Wadham said.

Charlie raised his gun and the three bodyguards

raised theirs too, all pointed at Charlie.

'Not until you kill me, Paul,' Charlie responded.

'I think that is long overdue,' he said. 'However, we seemed to have reached an impasse.'

The door to the courtyard was open, but there was no way to get there, as the men were directly in front of them.

'Fucking kill 'em!'

'Do 'em in! They're disgusting!'

The sound of the girls shouting from the other room, broke the silence.

Wadham's brow furrowed, he looked angry.

'Deal with that, will you.' He nodded at the bodyguard to his left, who barged past the men in front of him, and into the long room.

There was the sound of automatic gunfire, followed by the screams of children. Then silence.

'No!' Charlie launched himself at Wadham, smashing his face with the gun, beating him and beating him.

He was pulled off by the other two henchmen.

'Take him to the lock up downstairs!' Wadham shouted, wiping blood and spittle from his face.

'No, don't do that,' a voice came from beyond him in the courtyard. 'Put him down.'

DCI Jackson stood in the courtyard with a number of armed response personnel.

Charlie released himself from the men's grip.

'Got him?' Jackson asked Charlie.

'Yes. Yes, we've got him.'

The armed policemen rounded up the two henchmen and just as they were about to grab Wadham, he pulled out the small pistol from his suit pocket, raised the gun to the underside of his chin, and pulled the trigger.

'No!' Charlie screamed, but it was too late, as Paul Wadham collapsed in a broken heap on the floor in the dark corridor.

30

Charlie lifted the newspaper from the desk and took a large swig of his black coffee.

Dark. Complex. Sharp. He would have to remember this brand of coffee, a new one from Harris and Hoole.

Charlie was pleased to notice that the front page did not hold the Border Facility story.

It appeared, however, on page five, 'Explosion at Border Facility in Kent.'

Charlie huffed derisively.

'What's that, hun?' Tara asked as she moved around the kitchen, preparing toast.

'This…' Charlie said, pointing at the article.

Tara looked over his shoulder and read the article.

'This is unbelievable. "A gas leak caused an explosion, where one of the directors, Paul Wadham, sadly perished… along with a number of illegal immigrants who also died… it is unknown whether the facility will remain open…" well it's not what you know, eh?'

Charlie nodded sagely. He had already told Tara about the job, what he found, how it ended.

'Oh… "Wolfire declined to comment,"…' Charlie spoke dryly.

Tara turned and gave him a wry smile.

At that moment, her phone buzzed and she reached to get it a little too quickly. Charlie looked up from the paper.

'Think it's just my aunt, she wants to meet for coffee, before the next stage of lockdown...'

Charlie nodded. The government had hinted that new lockdown restrictions would start on Monday. Well at 9.13am on Wednesday morning, still no confirmation of it. Hythe Road was as busy as ever and the MPs were doing what they seemed to do best... dither.

Talking about me? □ the message read. Troy Wood... *again.*

Tara took a deep breath, placed her phone in her pocket and sat down at the table.

Normally, she would be terrified that an ex... friend, hardly a boyfriend, a man she had a passionate kiss with one night after too many vodkas...was spying on her.

She realised it was an incredibly creepy, weird thing to do... but she didn't feel threatened. She didn't know why. There was a three way pull that she felt, like three men holding a large sheet and it was bobbing her up and down keeping her afloat.

Charlie... the man she loved, but a man she was wary of, that she didn't fully trust... Troy Wood... a man who loved her, was there and who wanted her time and devotion.... And finally her unborn baby... her hope for a better, safer future.

Like the men holding the sheet, as the three of them got closer together, she felt like she was bobbing less, like she was in danger of falling and crashing to the ground, of the triumvirate coming apart.

'Did you read through the documents?' Tara asked, sipping a steaming cup of tea.

'Hm. You don't want to know,' Charlie said.

'I do, Charlie.' Tara said, staring at him across the table. She didn't smile, her tone was abrupt.

Charlie contemplated telling her where to stick it, but he wondered whether it was fair to share some information with his girlfriend, but not all. He put the paper down and grabbed the folder.

'Have you heard of Lacwear Company?' he asked.

'The home furnishings lot?'

'Yes, I believe so.'

'Of course, yeah. They are massive. Proper expensive though. I think it's ridiculously overpriced. My mum bought a lamp from there once.' Tara mused.

'You sure that's what she bought?'

'What do you mean, Charlie?'

'I mean are you sure that what arrived was a lamp and not something else?'

Tara paused and her brow furrowed.

'They were selling… humans?'

Charlie nodded tentatively. A collective pause.

'LAC…. Looked after children. Lacwear. They found young children who were taken in by the state, orphans, homeless, parents in jail. They were easier to find, no-one asking questions, kids who slipped through the cracks in the system. They scooped them up and kept them there and sold them to the highest bidder.'

'No... no way...' Tara's hand moved to her mouth, but Charlie wanted to expose the truth, he wanted to batter out the last of her naiveté, her innocence and show her what the real world was like.

'There was a code. All designed for the elite, the rich bods, the establishment, the likes of Wadham and your mate Wood...'

'Well, Troy is hardly part of the-'

'-Really, Tara? Are you going to stick up for him?' Charlie said, the temper in his voice rising.

'No, but... Jesus!'

'Sofia Chairs.... Lucia cushions.... A fucking *Erika* table... five grand, seven, ten. You weren't buying furniture, you bought kids. Kids that didn't fucking matter; to them, the state, to anyone. Folkestone kids, immigrants without parents off the boat, anyone. Bought and paid for peanuts, sold to the highest bidder. They were hiding it in plain sight. A perfect bloody crime.'

'It's disgusting.'

'That we agree on.'

There was silence between them. The time when they were lovers seemed far gone. They were now like two wolves prowling around the same den. Either trying to co-exist, or go for one another.

'As for Troy Wood, you know he is in on this, don't you?' Charlie probed.

Tara harrumphed. 'So you tell me…'

'I do tell you, yes, because it's true. You saw the letter, he predicted this chaos, lockdown, the whole shebang…'

'Maybe he's a modern-day Nostradamus…' Tara said nonchalantly.

'Are you trying to be funny?'

'Look, Charlie. I know him as a teacher from the girl's school. It's been a mad year or so where, according to you, he's now head of some religious templar paedophile order!' She said giggling to herself.

Charlie stared across the table at the woman who he loved. He barely recognised her anymore. From true love to utter disdain.

Charlie got up from his seat and left the room. He got changed, grabbed his wallet, phone and keys and headed out of the door.

'Charlie, wait… I'm just… it's…'

The door slammed behind him and Tara was left sitting at the table.

She wept. An explosion of red-faced, snot and tears. And she couldn't stop.

What was she doing? Pushing away the man she loved, and for what?

Tara took herself up to bed with a glass of water and lay down.

The pain of her pregnancy had truly kicked in.

She sent a message to Charlie, it just read:

sorry x.

****

Charlie hadn't heard from Robbie in a little while. He liked to fall off the radar every now and again it seemed.

Charlie didn't pester him about what he was doing, it was none of his business, but he could do with some company and a friend right now.

It was a twenty-minute walk to Ashford International train station from his house in Willesborough, but in Charlie's fervour it took him fifteen minutes. There was an inbound HS1 heading out to Folkestone, so he jumped on it and sat down.

He checked his phone, which he realised he hadn't done since yesterday afternoon. He was pleased when this happened. Not because he wanted to appear aloof, but because he enjoyed not being reliant on his mobile devices. There was a freedom he felt without them.

He had texts from Maddie, Jo, Jackson, Trev and Tara.

He ignored Tara and went straight to Maddie's:

Dad, are we going to football at the weekend? X

Charlie had decided they were going to go, earlier in the week. They both had season tickets and to be honest, he felt it was probably best to spend time away from Tara, given the way they were bickering. He didn't want to put Maddie in the middle of some passive-aggressive sniping. Been there, done that, bought the t-shirt. Thanks.

Jo's text was nice and perfunctory: *Pick up, Maidstone services- 4,30pm, Friday – drop off Sunday, 4.30pm.*

Hope you're well too, Jo. He thought to himself. Still though, it was Thursday afternoon, so not long before his daughter would be here. A momentary wave of joy washed over him.

Jackson's and Trev's texts were both similar, inviting Charlie to call at the earliest convenience.

He hated calling on the train, as the reception had a habit of dropping out, so he waited.

He wondered, given recent events who he would call first, it was an interesting conundrum. Jackson probably, he had been watching Charlie from afar and risked his own life, limb, reputation, to bust into the facility and rescue him.

He had done a good thing. It almost made up for dropping the case against Wadham and Wood. Almost. Anyway, Charlie would have done the same for him.

Trev was a canny character. He had definitely become a friend, but his motives were a little unclear. Was he just a renegade against the establishment, a rebel without a clue? It was difficult to say.

The train pulled into Folkestone Central and Charlie made the short walk to Junction 13 for a pint.

There was a different barman this time, a man he had recognised from somewhere before.

He walked towards him and he spoke.

'Hey, Charlie! Long time, no see!'

Charlie remembered from the voice, it was Nick from the Ward's Hotel.

'Hey, aren't you behind the wrong bar?' Charlie returned.

'Moved jobs. It wasn't going well at the Wards and the owner of this place is a friend, so trying a few shifts. What can I get for you?'

Charlie looked down at the pumps and noticed his personal favourite was on, 'Killer on The Loose.' Charlie pointed at it and took his jacket off, while Nick began pouring.

He took a deep gulp of the pint before making his way outside to call Jackson.

'About time, what have you been up to?' Jackson sounded rattled on the other end of the line.

'Well, arguing with T, trying to relax, failing… so… yeah…'

'Are you out drinking, Charlie?'

'I'm just having a couple, chill your beans. Eh, don't want to be a prick about it but… you know… you're not my boss anymore…'

'Oh, but it's still all right for me to come and save your arse, when you need it, eh?'

Jackson was right. Charlie had no right to give

him attitude.

'Yeah, about that, I really wanted to say thank you, Jacko. What you did for me was-' Charlie started.

'-Save it. I have new intel. Reliable intel about your good mate, Troy Wood…'

'I'm listening…'

'Same source that told me you are about to get cut to pieces again at the facility… so…'

'OK…'

'Football match, this weekend. Your mob against…'

'Burnley FC.'

'Right. Expected to be a sell-out, plus another thirty thousand through the doors of Westfield, to add to the shenanigans in East London. A real festival of bodies.'

'OK, I don't fully understand what you are getting at boss…' Charlie said.

'It seems Wolfire did not take kindly to the attack on the Facility. As I heard it, 'Wood is spitting feathers and spewing about it.' What you don't know is that in addition to Wadham and Lacwear's little side project… they were using those fuckers in there to test the virus and new vaccines.'

'As you predicted?'

'That's right. Did you ever wonder why they were sorted into their requisite ages and so on? They were testing various different antidotes to the pathogen.'

'On non-consenting humans?'

'Yes. On humans that don't matter. Not in the eyes of the British Government.'

'This goes that high?'

There was a pause. Despite Jackson buying a new untraceable device for these calls, he was still wary.

'I didn't say that. But…'

'Jeez… so let me guess, Wolfire are doing security at the London Stadium…'

'Correct…'

'And they are going to release the virus at the match…'

'Very good…'

'But due to what was happening at the facility, the bigwigs, government, Wolfire lot already have their vaccine sorted?'

'Well, it is about 92% 'sorted'. Thanks to your little sojourn over there, they hadn't quite finished their research.'

'Hence why Wood is pissed? Right. So, release the virus and bring London to its knees, that's Wood's plan?'

'It won't just bring London to its knees, it will kill thousands of its citizens and bring the world to its knees, change it forever. It's the perfect storm. Let's say a majority of people take a week or two weeks to develop symptoms… how many people will the average Londoner come into contact with in that time?'

'Not to mention tourists, travellers,

businessman… it will spread like wildfire…' Charlie mused. 'Is this why the 'lockdown' has been postponed? It was supposed to start this week, wasn't it?'

'If I were a betting man, Charlie, and I am, I would say that is a strong possibility. It could also be because our prime minister is a dithery old toff too, but either way, this is potentially the last day where these types of gatherings can occur. Honestly, if this goes off, it will be brutal out there. No-one talking or socialising, bars and pubs closed never to return, masks every time you leave the house. Not to mention dear old Auntie Ethel, she will be going bye bye. The new strain of the virus has lethal effects on the elderly.' Jackson stated.

Charlie took another slug of his pint and put it on one of the outside tables. He wondered what the demographic at West Ham was. There must have been at least 25% over 60's, maybe more.

'You know I am supposed to be at the match, right?' Charlie stated to Jackson.

'Yes, I predicted as much. Well, you're definitely going now.'

'I am supposed to be taking Maddie.'

'Take her, it will act as the perfect decoy. Wolfire will be expecting some intervention, from their arch-nemesis. Taking a minor will throw them from your scent.'

'Are you mad, I'm not risking her!'

'Think about it, Charlie…'

Charlie thought about the Facility. All of the enclosed cells housing just one adult each. Why? Because they were infected... and the girls were housed all together...

'Right, so the young are immune.'

'God, Charlie you are good. You would make a fine police officer!'

'I would consider it, if the force weren't so corrupt, Jacko!'

'Ouch, Charlie. That hurts. I'm trying to do my best here.'

'Yes, and I am grateful. This is what I signed up for. This is the type of work I need. Catching criminals, terrorists, the bad guys.'

'I've known you long enough not to get sentimental with you. Every time I give you my heart, you trample all over it.'

Charlie sniggered at his old boss' tongue in cheek comments.

'On that note, I have your voluntary redundancy package here. Shall I email it over to you, as you requested?'

Charlie hesitated.

'Let's wait. See how this play's out.'

Charlie could sense Jackson's smile through the phone.

'I have another call, boss. Got to run.'

'See you later, buddy.'

Charlie put the phone down and picked up the new call.

'Trev, how's it going?'

'You heard the news yet?' Trev said perfunctorily.

'West Ham?'

'Yes. Not good.'

'Not good at all. I am on it, want to help me devise a plan for it?' Charlie asked.

'Way ahead of you, buddy. Meet me at mine.'

'Here, Trev. Before you go. The kids, a little birdie says, they're immune from the virus?'

'Your little birdy is right.'

'Do you know why?'

'Unsure at this stage… possibly something to do with other injections they take like MMR, providing immunity. Something like that.'

'I see. You reckon that's true though?'

'I reckon I haven't seen a child get it, so it seems very likely. Get to mine as soon as you can.'

The line went dead.

Charlie finished his drink and took the short walk towards Central Folkestone.

When he reached Trev's block, he was buzzed in and entered the delipidated flat and sat in the only seat in the room that was available. Trev was behind his desk, watching the CCTV videos that sat to the left of his desk, while lighting a cigarette.

'So…' Charlie said.

'One second, Charlie…' Trev said, placing his fingers on the laptop keyboard, whilst watching the camera in the top right.

He waited for a man to skulk shadily towards a set of double doors, the man approached, and tentatively pressed a button, presumably for entry.

As he did, Trevor pressed three keys on the laptop simultaneously, and the man seemed to be shocked, crumpling in half and eventually falling to the floor.

Trev took a drag on his cigarette and turned to face Charlie.

'It works!' he said, with a wide grin and large eyes.

'Err… what works?' Charlie asked.

'Never you mind, Charlie me boy. Right, Saturday.'

'Yes, how do you know about it?'

'A lady never tells Charlie, let's just say this has been 'leaked.' Not full scale, but those in the know, know. It's a fucking shit show. Not good.'

'The master of the understatement, Trev.'

'If they release this virus, in that area on Saturday… it will tear through the city in a matter of days. The death toll will be nothing like we have ever seen before.'

'I know. So, what are we going to do?'

'Well, ask not what I can do for you, but what you can do for this great nation…'

'Oh, I see. You're not coming again?' Charlie asked, slightly irate at Trev's non-committal attitude to the actual action.

Trev met Charlie's glare, his eyes wide like an

angry bear.

'I mean it's OK, if you can't…'

Trev fished out some photos beneath the piles of papers on his desk.

'Right, so they will be bringing the virus in a special suitcase that keeps it at the optimum temperature. They will then give the individual amounts to the Wolfire guards. So, your best bet is to intercept the virus before it reaches the guards.'

'This sounds unlikely…'

'Unlikely? Charlie, its nigh on impossible. But the consequences are really unthinkable. And anyway, we have the best man on the job.'

'Hm. Yeah, right. Why can't we go in hard, armed response, maybe?'

'The minute Wolfire knows they've been rumbled, they'll release it. It's got to be covert.'

'What about Maddie…getting spotted?'

Trev leaned back in his seat, deep in thought.

'I think the issue with your daughter is moot. If you take her, you will have more cover and are less likely to get spotted. Let's face it Charlie, the game is going to happen and no-one is going to know the difference either way. This is a silent threat.'

Charlie didn't want to use his daughter as a pawn, and would not put her in danger again.

However, he didn't want her to miss out on the game, trying to explain to her that she couldn't go, would be far worse. Plus, all the research suggested that children were immune from this thing.

'I am going to be in your ear, Charlie. I can guide you to the virus, intercept it, and you can pass it on to me. Then straight back to Maddie as if nothing ever happened.' Trev continued.

It was bold, it was madness. It might just work.

31

'So, there is good news and bad news…'

'Please tell me we are going to the match?' Maddie said, clutching her hands together, and bouncing on her tiptoes.

'Yes, we are going to the match…'

'Yes!' Maddie turned and fist-pumped.

'But I am technically 'at work' when I'm there, so I am going to have to leave-'

'-Oh, that's all-right dad, I have organised to meet up with Jacob and his dad anyway. You know, the ones we talk to in the block next to us?' Maddie had developed Jo's incredibly annoying habit of finishing off his sentences for him. That said, he was quite pleased with what she said.

'Well, that's good. I'm going to ring Jacob's dad and make sure he is happy to watch you for a while, but I will be gone for part of the start.'

'Don't worry dad, it's West Ham! It will be fine. Like you always say, it's one big family! Technically, I could make it home on my own, if I needed to,' she said. 'Remember, you told me how to do it last time.'

'Think you still remember?'

'Of course. Out of the stadium, across the bridge, down to Marks and Spencer's and follow the signs to Stratford International. The Ashford train always goes from the same platform.'

'Which one?'

'Erm…the one we always go to?'

Charlie and his daughter both smiled at one another.

'Yes, well I am glad you feel so confident, Mad. Still, don't go anywhere except where we normally go in the stadium, OK? Jacob, our seat and the toilet in Block 130, got it?'

'Got it!' she said, with a big grin across her face. 'Now can we get ready please?'

Charlie could see his little girl was growing up. The years had passed since he first split from Jo, and his primary fear was losing Maddie, losing her for good. Drifting into the Folkestone night, and her in the pleasant lands of middle England.

Looking back, he couldn't quite believe how it had panned out. How had he done it? Forge bonds that now could not be broken? Presence. As a father that is your only weapon in the war of divorce.

Stay hungry, stay free, stay around.

Charlie went to put on his utility belt, with space for a knife and a small baton, but realised he was a spectator at a game.

There was no protection from the badge and nothing to hide behind. He had to do this alone and he wasn't quite sure what he was walking into. This was Charlie Stone's biggest test.

'Right, dad… I'm ready!' Maddie jumped into the room, with her West Ham top and beanie on. Her hoodie was wrapped around her waist and she had a pair of Nike trainers on.

'OK, you look great. That hoodie needs to go on and you are going to need a jacket too.'

'But, dad...'

'Do you want to have this conversation with your stepmum?' Maddie, knowing she would get shorter thrift with Tara, exhaled and left the room.

'You've got five minutes!' Charlie called behind her. 'See you downstairs.'

'You guys off?' Tara asked as Charlie bounded down the steps.

'Yes, sweet,' he kissed her on the cheek, but chose against the hug. Tara's belly had been a bit painful in the past few days.

'OK, well have fun, ring me at half time or something.'

'Sure thing. Maddie, come on!' Charlie shouted up.

'Just coming…' after a shuffle, Maddie appeared in the hallway with her West Ham top pulled over her hoodie and her jacket.

'Good effort!' Charlie said.

'I know, right? See you, T!' Maddie called.

'Have fun, be good, don't be too late.'

They walked along Hythe Road in the winter sunshine and towards the town centre.

'Do you think Antonio will play today?' Maddie asked.

'Hm… I think so, we haven't got any other forward options, but it's a bit of a risk with his hamstrings…'

'I really hope he plays…'

'Would you say he's your favourite?'

'Yeah, definitely.'

'And then?'

'Hm.' Maddie paused. 'Rice probably. Or Noble. Or Snoddy… Scottish milk from Scottish cows!'

I wasn't quite sure where that had come from, but Maddie loved saying it in her best Scottish accent whenever Robert Snodgrass' name came up.

'About Snoddy… he may be moving to West Brom…'

'No! That's not right. This will be the last time I can say, Scottish milk from Scottish cows to him!'

They both laughed.

Charlie thought to himself how life may, just may, work out OK. Tara seemed more relaxed. Maddie was back. They were a family again.

Charlie thought once more about the mission. He checked his earpiece was in the inside pocket of his jacket and he decided he would put that together on the train up. It may look suspicious to some people, but they would probably just assume he was a security guard at Westfield or the match.

He checked his phone to see if Robbie had returned any of his calls. He hadn't.

Charlie took a deep breath and put his arm around his daughter.

■■

After Charlie and Maddie had left, Tara had returned to bed. She tossed and turned, or at least as much as she could, given the large round ball which protruded from her stomach.

She wished Charlie could be here, to lay in bed, to hold her, to tell her they were going to be OK. That they would get through this moment, this tension, just fine.

Instead, the mail landed on the mat with a thud. *Something heavy,* Tara thought.

She heaved herself up and waddled downstairs to the front door. She bent down slowly at the knees, (from the hips wasn't possible), and picked up the two letters and the small package wrapped in brown paper that was on the floor.

She placed the letters to one side and took the hand-delivered package upstairs. It just said T on it, Tara's nickname.

She sat on the bed and ripped it open, revealing a letter and a number of photographs.

One showed Charlie holding a gun, his face maniacal, another was of him and another woman, she had her face buried in his neck and she was naked apart from a towel.

The final photograph was Charlie, with a group of naked girls, hugging one of them.

Tara didn't need to read the accompanying letter, it was like an epiphany.

This had to end.

32

'Jacob's not on this train, he comes in on a different one I think,' Maddie said, playing with her phone.

The beauty of getting the train from Ashford to London, rather than Folkestone, is that the journey only took around thirty minutes and there was a more regular service.

The downside was that you could rarely get a seat.

Fortunately, one happy hammer insisted on moving out of his seat to let Maddie sit down, while Charlie stood beside her.

He removed the ear piece as subtly as he could from its packaging, before placing it in his ear. He connected it to his phone via Bluetooth and connected with Trevor, who was waiting on the other end.

'What's the score in the early kick off, dad?' Maddie asked, looking up from her phone.

'I'm unsure, sweetheart,' Charlie said. Maddie noticed the earpiece in his ear and looked concerned.

'It's just for work,' he mouthed a nervous smile and Maddie went back to her phone.

The train glided through the Kentish countryside and then into the Medway towns, a brief highlight for Charlie was seeing the river that separated the men of Kent from the Kentish men, and Rochester Castle standing proud in the distance.

For all its faults, he loved his home county. He knew it like the back of his hand, just like London.

The train was bathed in claret and blue. A large swathe of bodies joined at Ebbsfleet International. Groups of lads, groups of girls, dads and their daughters, full of hope and totally oblivious to the evil forces that were silently at work.

He knew that he needed to intercept this case to ensure that the lives of these people, his people, would be saved.

Onwards towards the Dartford Bridge which Charlie always marvelled at, before down under the river and then into deepest, darkest East London. Factories, car manufacturers, boggy marshes. The arse end of London, the industrial gulch that powers the shiny, new cosmopolitan London of 2021.

The train eventually pulled into Stratford International and the pair exited, along with hundreds of other fans. As usual, they walked to the end of the platform, past the first escalator, the stairs and the lift, all the way down to the final travelator which was usually pretty empty.

Then it was over the road into Westfield, up the stairs and across towards the eateries and pubs.

'Are we going to stop for a drink, dad?'

Charlie checked his watch, 2.20pm.

'Sure, hun. Just a quick one.'

They snuck between the crowds and towards the Holiday Inn, where there was a bar on the third floor.

It was busy with fans, but not unbearably so, unlike The Cow or The Bat and Ball. The downside was a pint of Guinness was £7.20. That said, Charlie wasn't planning on drinking at all today, so in then end he opted for an apple juice, the same as Maddie.

'Dad, can you check the team?'

Charlie did.

'Good news, Antonio is... playing!'

'Yes!' Maddie said, holding out her hand for a high five, which Charlie duly accepted.

'Hey, Charlie? Charlie? Can you hear me?' the voice crackled in his earpiece.

'Oh, hey, Trev.'

'Ah, good. You can hear me. I see you're in Westfield... Holiday Inn is it?'

'Correct. A pre-match drink, for the nerves...' Charlie returned.

Maddie looked up and smiled at him as Charlie pointed and made a yawning face, indicating his work commitments.

'Charlie, I have intercepted some comms from Wolfire HQ, it looks like they are collecting the virus just after kick off. As soon as the whistle goes for the start of the match, you are going to need to come out.'

'Right.'

'At the West Entrance, by the player's entrance,

there will be a Wolfire Security van that brings it…'

Charlie got up from his chair and walked towards the toilet.

'Difficult to get down there, Trev…'

'Yes, so I have an executive pass stashed for you, just near Gate D. I'll send you the co-ordinates.'

'D, that's where all the food and drink outlets are… it will be rammed down there…'

'Exactly, Charlie. Hiding in plain sight.'

'Hm. OK, anything else?'

'Get down to the corporate entrance, under the stadium by 3.15pm, the rest is up to you.'

'Right, thanks.'

'Don't worry, buddy. It will all be fine.'

The line went dead, Charlie washed his hands and went back out.

'Right, Mad. Time to go.'

The walk to the ground was normally one of Charlie's favourite parts of the matchday experience. Today, understandably, he was filled with nerves. He put on a brave face as he walked through the fans, past the coppers and the programme sellers and towards the security checks.

'Did you message Jacob?' Charlie asked.

'Yeah, he is here. Already in his seat.'

'Awesome. Dad's got to go just after kick off, so let's see if we can sit next to them from the start.'

Maddie nodded, despite each game being a sell-out, somehow there were always empty seats dotted around. In their block, a number of groups had clearly bought season tickets and regularly didn't come, so there were often spare seats. It's simple to move people around or let kids down the front so they can see better.

Once through security, Charlie and Maddie queued up at the chip stand.

Pulling out his phone, he checked the co-ordinates that Trev had sent him. They signalled a point that was under two minutes walk from his current location.

Charlie placed a tenner into Maddie's hand and told her he'd be back shortly.

He moved towards the GPS signal, which was a few vans further down, behind an orange ice cream van overlooking the river that flowed serenely beneath the hordes.

Charlie could see a brown envelope attached to the back of the van, so swiftly grabbed it as conspicuously as he could and headed back to Maddie.

Drinks and food secured, they went through Gate E and towards their block.

Their block was relatively empty, as often fans didn't arrive until the match had started.

'There they are, dad!' Maddie said excitedly, seeing her school friend above them.

She ran up the steps and the two of them hugged, while Charlie shook Jacob's father's hand. They had met before and exchanged numbers, but this time Charlie found out his name was Wilf and they live in Tonbridge.

London Calling boomed through the sound system and the players were on the pitch. The kids were buzzing and the crowds started to flow in more steadily.

Charlie looked around the large stadium.

'I'm forever blowing bubbles...'

The thousands of people.

'Pretty bubbles in the air...'

The lives at stake.

'They fly so high...'

Maddie nudged her dad to raise his hands and sing with her and he duly obliged.

The sound was electrifying as it always was in those opening moments. Sixty-thousand people united as one.

The whistle blew and Charlie took a deep breath.

'I'll be back, all right?' Charlie said, kissing Maddie on the cheek.

'Sure, dad! It's fine, I'll see you in a bit!'

Charlie nodded at Wilf, Jacob's Dad, and thanked him for watching Maddie and then jogged back up the concrete stairs.

33

Charlie was walking against the crowd, but he made it back outside to the walkway around the arena.

The outside area was still fairly populated by smokers and drinkers. The old guard who came more for the crack with their mates, rather than the experience at the London Stadium.

'Are you there, Charlie?' Trev spoke into his ear.

'Yep, making my way around now.'

'OK, that's good, the van will arrive in the next few minutes.'

Charlie felt a wave of nausea… or was it fear? Excitement? He wasn't sure, but his heart was pounding and his legs felt as though he was walking on air.

'Ere wait up, sweetcheeks!'

It was a voice Charlie recognised all too well. Deep, gruff, estuary.

Charlie turned to see Robbie's rotund frame jogging towards him.

'Robbie, I've been trying to call you. Where have you been?'

'Hiding in the shadows, pal.'

Charlie looked at him and they both started laughing.

'I couldn't let my man go into battle without his partner, eh?' he continued.

'Well, good to know. Although I don't know if you are going to get in…'

'What into the game, I wouldn't want to watch that shower of shit if you paid me!'

Robbie was a die-hard Chelsea fan.

'No, I mean the corporate part… where we need to be.'

'Trev gave me one of these,' Robbie held up the executive pass.

'Sweet. Although they aren't going to let a ruffian like you in there, mate.'

'Bollocks! They would be lucky to have me.'

The men continued the walk past the club shop and the away fans entrance.

'OK, you need to get down the stairs, Charlie…' Trev said into his ear. 'Then you are going to the left of the tent…' Trev continued.

'Are you sure, I'm pretty certain the entrance is through the tent…'

'Nah, trust me, Charlie… head around the corner… and you should see the van about ten metres ahead.'

Charlie trusted the voice in his ear and as he came down the steps and turned to his left, he noticed the Wolfire van. It was nearer than he anticipated, so he stopped and ducked down near the stairs.

Charlie looked up to see where Robbie was, but he was no longer there. He must have got caught up the top briefly, or nipped into the toilet. Charlie thought it best to wait for his pal.

'No, Charlie, come around the side of the scase and come directly forward. You can hide in there…' Trev said.

Charlie followed the instruction, came around the corner and walked into the alcove. It was a dead end, Charlie turned to see Trev in front of him.

'Hi, Charlie,' another familiar voice to his left. This time it was Jimmy, his protégé from Folkestone Police Station. Charlie knew there was a rat.

It was the last thing Charlie heard before the taser went into the side of his body and he disappeared into darkness, crumpling on the floor.

Trevor beckoned two Wolfire guards from the van to assist Jimmy in picking up Charlie's withered body and placing it in the back of the van.

34

'Are you OK, Tara?'

There was silence, she stared straight ahead.

'Tara?'

Her solemn face staring.

'T?'

Her eyes on the horizon. Charlie gave up.

The beach was red, probably blood. Everything seemed to have a touch of blood in it.

Charlie looked over at his fiancée. She was further away now. Her jaw opened and stretched; her teeth were falling out.

'Oh, is this hell?'

She looked straight ahead. Nodded.

'I see. Are we OK, T? I really hope we can be OK, you know? I'm sorry.'

He turned to face her and she had disappeared.

'Literally, hook line and sinker. The silly prick!'

Charlie could hear them talking and carrying him. He was aching. Black bag on his head.

'He is waking up, I think.'

'Oops, not yet, big time Charlie!'

One of Wolfire's infantry cracked him on the head with the butt of his rifle.

Charlie was back in the stadium. Empty.

Empty, except for Maddie. Across the other side.

'Maddie!'

She couldn't hear him. His heart beat faster.

'Mad!'

Two figures, men, were walking down the steps towards her. She couldn't see them.

'Maddie!'

She was oblivious.

Sitting on her own in the stadium. Looking solemn. Wondering where her dad is.

The men sat down next to her. They talked to her. She gets up as they get up. She walks with them. The men from Wolfire.

Cold water splashed over Charlie's face.

He came too. His body ached all over

The room was white. Surgical.

There were clear plastic coverings on the floors and the walls. Charlie was tied to two brackets on the floor.

It was cold. Why did he ache so much?

'Did anyone ever tell you the story of the two wolves, Charlie?' It was Trevor's voice.

Charlie's eyes were still blurry. He blinked to regain focus, but it was taking time. The light was bright, industrial.

'The two wolves. It is an old, Native American proverb. Of course, no-one cares about the Native Americans anymore. Wiped out by small pox, greed and fucking Americans...'

His arms were tied by something tight and sharp. His sight was returning.

He could see two figures, two men he knew.

'Inside every person sits two wolves. A good

wolf and a bad wolf. Depending on which wolf you feed, is the wolf that will win. If you starve one of the wolves, the other one feeds. What do you think of that, Charlie?'

Charlie could hear knives being sharpened. The Carver.

'Charlie? You must have an opinion? You have an opinion on everything else?'

Charlie wriggled as a figure moved closer. There he was, topless, black combat trousers. A metal table of implements to his right-hand side, as he circled the large room.

'I like it. It's simple. Life is simple. You see for me, I never really had the good wolf. It was starved from a young age. My father, he took the good wolf and he beat it, he burned it, he fucked it and left it for dead. So, the bad wolf grew. Now it's all I know.'

In one swift movement, The Carver launched at Charlie and sliced in sweeping movements across Charlie's back.

The pain pulsed through his body to his brain. Charlie screeched in agony.

'Ah, there he is... the good wolf dying...'

Trevor left through a door in the back room and there was silence, but for blood dripping on the plastic sheet across the floor.

The Carver sliced again across Charlie's back, this time back and forth, back and forth through the thin t-shirt that covered him.

He was going to die here if he couldn't do

something.

'If you're going to cut me up, look at me when you do it. If you're such a fucking psycho.' Charlie spat.

'The bad wolf speaks...' The Carver whispered.

'You're a fucking coward. With your knives. Cutting up tired, old coppers.'

The Carver picked up a knife and threw it. It sped through the air and hit Charlie square in the shoulder, he yelped.

Tears formed in Charlie's eyes.

'Maddie,' he whispered.

'Ah, yes. Who knows where she is, where she might be now...'

The Carver came closer to Charlie.

'Don't cry. You have had this coming. For years, Charlie...'

Where the hell was Robbie? He was just there when I got kidnapped? Charlie thought to himself.

'You're going to die here, Charlie.' The Carver said quietly.

Charlie nodded, grateful for the chance of peace.

'Yes. Come, come here,' Charlie said through the tears, through the sweat on his face.

The Carver came forward, a large machete in his hand.

He looked pityingly at his prey.

'Please, come here...' Charlie asked.

'A dying man's final wish?' The Carver said.

'Please just hold me...' Charlie said through the floods of tears, that just wouldn't stop. He was nearly there now. Redemption. Forgiveness. The end.

'Oh, embrace it, Charlie…' The Carver said, kneeling next to him and putting his arm around his shoulder, a brief moment of understanding, of synergy, through the cruelty.

Like lightning, Charlie thrust his body sidewards, launching at The Carver, his open mouth towards his larynx.

For a moment, the two men were caught in the moment until the Carver fell forwards, the knife falling from his hand and across the tarpaulin floor.

Charlie was now the predator and he had his subject on the ground, his jaw clamped around his throat.

His eyes maniacal, his mind focused. Not letting go until his last breath was drawn.

The teeth sank deeper into the flesh, Charlie pushed his full weight further down onto the windpipe.

The Carver's legs wriggled in protest, but it was only a matter of time until it was done.

The bad wolf.

He used his feet to pull the knife towards him and he manoeuvred himself over it to cut his hands free. He got up and made his way to the door. It was metal and locked from the inside.

Charlie opened it, using keys from the Carvers trousers, and found himself in a larger warehouse building. He managed to walk faster, but couldn't run due to the excruciating pain across his back.

Once at the other end, another door, which he came through and melted into the bright light of daytime London. Somewhere in the east.

He didn't recognise it, but his only motivation was to find a phone.

The road was quiet, industrial. No-one around. No phone boxes anymore. Blood, dripping on the floor. Charlie's legs were failing.

'I need a phone,' he said, to no-one in particular. 'A phone! Someone help me!'

35

'This is the last time I talk to you before you are going to have to stay here permanently. You do know that don't you?'

'Do you think so?'

Dad smiled.

'This is really the last time…'

'It's time, I think.'

'You and your thoughts, son. Look where they've got you, eh?'

'Well, that's your fault, I guess.'

'You have your own life, son. You can't keep bemoaning your past. History. Listen to me. Do you remember that time I'd moved to Slade Green? I was in the Capri. The Spaghetti Incident was on in the car?'

'Yes.'

'You were fourteen and you were scared.'

'Yes.'

'Did I say it was going to be all right?'

Silence.

'Same year I reckon, 1995. We were watching England South Africa, cricket. Allan Donald firing in, Shaun Pollock, Big Mac… do you remember?'

'Michael Atherton?'

'Exactly, son.'

'You wanted South Africa to win, dad.'

'I know. And what happened?'

'Atherton happened.'

'Exactly, son. That's the good wolf. Sticking in there. Hanging about. Presence. Not death. Not glory.

Glory comes from longevity. Being there.'
'You missed my wedding. My kid.'
'Exactly, son. Don't be like me.'
'But, I'm tired.'
'Everyone's tired. It's tiring. Fuck 'em. Fuck 'em all.
They're going to need you down there.'
'They are?'
'Well, she will.'
'Tara?'
'Ah, bad news about that… this is the last time. I'm
sorry, son. I don't want to see you here again.'
'Hm. Nothing changes.'

The beeping of the machine was comforting as Charlie slowly opened his eyes.

There was quiet, no-one was there. Just the sound of the machine.

Charlie was lying on his front, his head through a small hole, like the massage tables. His back open, raw and sore.

He tried to move his body; it wasn't listening.

He breathed in and out, in and out. A blessing.

He closed his eyes and drifted in and out of sleep for what seemed like hours. He couldn't be sure.

Charlie explored with his fingers and he found a small button by his right hand. He pressed it. Nothing happened.

He closed his eyes. Sleep. Blissful sleep.

'Mr Stone?'

Charlie tried to answer, but it was impossible.

He croaked and cracked.

'He's waking up,' there were quiet voices whispering. 'Mr Stone we are going to lean you back. OK?'

Again, Charlie couldn't speak.

There was a metal clunk and Charlie felt gravity shift his torso up and the room, the nurses, the world, spun past him, before he was able to regain his senses once more.

The nurse was pretty. He smiled. She smiled too.

'Hi, Mr Stone. There is some water. Here let me help you.'

The water was heavenly elixir, cold, sweet and refreshing in equal measure.

'You really are very tough, Mr Stone. They keep trying to kill you, but they can't can they?' the nurse smiled coyly.

Charlie's brow furrowed through his bandages and the nurse laughed.

'Here,' she passed him a newspaper. His coma was front page news.

'Maddie?' he uttered hopefully.

'Ah… we didn't think it would take long…'

The nurse made her way outside, Charlie waited nervously.

Did the nurse even know if Maddie was OK?

Through the frosted glass, he saw a lime green beanie bobbing up and down, around the corner and into the room. There she was, his girl, smiling ear to ear.

'Dad!'

'Hi, sweet,' he said, rubbing her hand as she came near to the bed.

'You look a mess!'

'How did you get back from the football?'

'Gosh, dad that was like a week ago... Jacob's dad took me... well he took me to the train station and put me on the train. I rang Tara and she picked me up from Ashford.'

Charlie nodded, smiled.

'Where am I?' Charlie asked.

The nurse was standing at the door. Maddie looked over, Charlie thought he could see Jo's unmistakable frame through the frosting.

'Hospital, Mr Stone. West London. But don't worry for now. You need to rest-'

'-Where's Tara?' Charlie asked.

Maddie looked at the ground.

'Shall we leave your dad to rest for now?' the nurse said, moving Maddie towards the door.

'Love you, dad. I bought you some chocolate and a football magazine to read.'

'Oh, you are an angel,' Charlie croaked.

'Dad, I'm sorry this keeps happening to you. I want to help you get the bad guys.'

'Don't worry, I'll.. I'll...' Charlie couldn't finish the sentence.

'Come on young lady, let's let your father get some more rest if he can,' the nurse ushered Maddie out of the room.

'See you soon!' Maddie blew a kiss from the doorway.

Charlie smiled.

'Rest, please, Mr Stone,' the nurse said, injecting him with something in his arm.

'What's th…' before he could get his words out, he had drifted into a mellow slumber.

Charlie awoke with a jolt. He had a feeling that someone was there. They were.

He opened his eyes, focus came quicker than before.

'Morning, Charlie,' the voice of DCI Jackson spoke.

'Morning,' Charlie croaked. Jackson passed him a paper cup of water.

'You are lucky to be alive. Again,' Jackson continued.

Charlie nodded.

'If you had been with us, Charlie… we could have helped you…' Jackson continued.

'You didn't want the case, Darren. And anyway, you had become so good at following me, I thought you might turn up at the last minute.'

'Yeah, I wish I had, looking at the state of you. Sometimes we actually have police work to do. Remember that, do you?'

Charlie finished the paper cup and placed it on the table.

'Are you ready to talk?' Jackson asked.

'Sure,' Charlie said. Still querying his surroundings. He presumed the injection before his sleep was morphine. There was an enormous sense of wellbeing. Charlie wasn't overly fussed where he was for now.

'We were in fact monitoring your whereabouts from Ashford up to the stadium. We had you the whole time, right up until kick off. As far as we were concerned, you were still in the stadium with Maddie. Your signal never moved...'

'I had Trevor in my earpiece. He was talking me through the events and so on. I didn't realise he was with Wolfire all along.'

'I see. So, it seems like through the connection to your phone, he jammed the GPS signal. Clever.'

'Yeah, he's good with shit like that. Comms, tech...' Charlie's voice was croaky and he found it difficult to talk.

'I have his profile here,' Jackson passed Charlie the iPad, but Charlie didn't take it. He looked at the picture, nodded, looked away.

'He was at the stadium with them. He was there, when I got taken away.'

'Taken away?'

Charlie took a deep breath. The door handle turned. A man in a white coat, who looked suspiciously like a psychologist padded in tentatively.

'Who's this?' Charlie said.

'Good morning, Charlie. I'm Doctor Pathon, Chief Psychologist at the Windsor Unit...'

Charlie had heard of this place. A high-level, secure psychiatric unit in Ealing.

'Right. OK, so why am I here?'

'Charlie, the doctor is going to sit in for now if that's OK. Just tell us the story of what happened.' Jackson said.

'I was in the stadium with Maddie. The plan was to go and intercept the virus at the stadium before they distributed it to the Wolfire security.'

The doctor scribbled furiously on his pad.

'I walked through the crowds, Trevor had told me that the van with the virus was down by the corporate entrance, he gave me a pass for it, I must have it somewhere…'

'Go on, Charlie…' Jackson urged.

'Yeah… then Robbie arrived. I hadn't heard from him in days, so I was glad to see him and he walked with me, but I lost him just before the steps down. When I got down the van was there, but also Trevor and Jimmy. I was tasered, blacked out. Woke up in the warehouse.'

The doctor continued to write. Jackson was frozen still. If you tried to move him, he would snap in half. No-one spoke.

'Where's Tara?' Charlie broke the silence.

'We are going to come to that, Charlie. Can we focus on this for now, mate?' Jackson asked.

'Is she OK?'

'Yes, yes. She's fine. Safe.' Jackson said.

Charlie nodded, trusting his old friend.

'Charlie can you tell me more about your friend, Robbie?' the doctor said, not looking up from his papers.

'I met him in Folkestone. I was drinking too

much. Suffering from the… a…. death of a friend. He was out and he liked to drink and have fun, so we became buddies.'

'Can you… elaborate on what you did with him?'

'Did with him… what is he-?'

'-No… no… sorry, my mistake. *Do*, with him, I meant.' The doctor corrected himself.

'All of it. He was with me for all of it; Thraxin, Wolfire and then then the stadium…' realising Charlie may have implicated himself in crimes, he shot a glance at Jackson, who nodded at Charlie and placed his hand on his shoulder.

He knew Charlie couldn't go into too much detail about what they had actually done together, in front of the doctor.

'Can we get to the important stuff, here? What's happened with Troy Wood, Wolfire?' Charlie asked, getting a little irate that the answers he wanted were not as forthcoming as he wished.

'I think it is best we talk about this at a time when you feel calm and are up to it. I'm going to go now, Charlie. But I will see you a little later. Maybe, leave him to rest for a bit?' the doctor aimed at Jackson, who nodded.

The doctor left and slowly closed the door behind him.

'What the fuck is going on, Jacko?'

Jackson was deep in thought, wondering where to start.

'The good news… your story made the press. I

mean when they found you, you had lost four pints of blood. They traced the story back to Wolfire, the dodgy operations. In your stuff we found the corporate ticket, the earpiece and your phone records with this… Trevor… who it turns out is part of the Wolfire 'elite' guard. So, that has shut their whole operation down.'

'No way! What about the virus?'

'Of course, it is impossible to know. When the story broke, they destroyed all documents, any paper trail. Wood disappeared off the face of the earth. That said, transmission of the virus has increased ten-fold in London and across the home counties, so it would suggest that those horrible bastards did release it, but we will never know.'

'But Wolfire is no more?'

'Correct. Their operations have been entirely shut down by the government. Details withheld, but they have taken the fall for it all: the virus, Lacwear scandal, testing on the immigrants. All of it dies with them.'

The men looked at each other. Jackson waited for a response that never came.

'Of course, we both know that it doesn't die with them. The same shit will carry on. More covert, more brutal, but the good news is we did what we could, and one tyrannical regime is gone.'

'To be replaced by another?'

'You have been in this long enough, Charlie, to know how it works. Nothing ever changes. You just have to keep doing the best you can, keep fighting the good fight, keep working hard… you know.'

'For what? For it to get covered up? For paedophiles to blow up kids they were selling and get away with it?'

Jackson paused. He was playing with his wedding ring, looking down at his hands.

Eventually he looked up.

'You know how it works, Charlie.'

He geared up to rant again, but stopped himself. The air had gone. The main sail down.

'Charlie, there is some bad news, though.'

'Are you taking the piss? Was that not the bad news?'

'No, not as such.'

Charlie's mind was spinning like the reels on a fruit machine. Jackpot.

'Fuck, the baby. The baby!'

'No, no! The baby is fine. She hasn't had it yet, but it's fine… she's fine.'

'But?'

'Tara has left you.' Jackson looked down at his hands again. 'Sorry.'

Charlie produced a wry smile.

'Can you blame her?' he said, a tear rolling down his face.

An answer never came.

36

'I thought we would be together forever?'
'That's what everyone thinks at the time.'
'But I thought that we were different.'
Pause.
'Charlie, everyone thinks that.'
'OK.'
It wasn't OK.
Charlie was back at the fairground.
He was seven years old. He could see Tara, at the top of the Ferris wheel, smiling down at him. Her hair was blowing in the wind. She looked magnificent.
'Are you my mum?'
Tara cocked her head and smiled.
'I don't want it to end. I am really sorry.'
'No-one wants it to end. But all things must end. This baby needs to be safe. It will be safe.'
'I wasn't there. Was I?'
Tara smiled; tears formed in her eyes. Her brown hair blew in the breeze.
Charlie licked his large lollipop.
He realised there was a hole in the bottom of his shorts. No-one could see it, but he knew it was there.
'I'm sorry.' Charlie said.
Tara was crying now.
'I'm sorry, too.'
She reached out towards the lost little boy and then she disappeared.

When Charlie woke, he was greeted by Doctor Pathon.

'Morning, Charlie,' the doctor said.

'Hi, doctor,' Charlie spoke.

He felt fairly chipper. The sun came through the blinds, he was healing and the doctor was clearly interested in his recovery.

Then as his mind flicked through his recent memories, he came crashing through the floors, back into the arms of his old friend, sadness.

'Charlie, I wanted to pick up some of the things we discussed yesterday if possible?'

Charlie nodded, if only to stop himself thinking of her.

'Obviously, we want to discuss… your friend… Robbie, in a little more detail if we can,' he continued. 'Do you know where he came from?'

'Yeah, Fulham. But he was a Chelsea fan.'

'Are you sure, I mean did you ever witness anything that could verify that?'

'Well, why would he lie?'

'Of course, but could you be sure of where he came from, for definite?'

'I mean, could I prove it? No.'

The doctor scribbled.

'And did you go to his place of residence in Folkestone?'

'Where he lived? No. We nearly did a couple of times, but never made it in the end.'

'I see.'

The doctor scribbled.

'So, you communicated really via-?'

'-We met up. We talked in pubs and bars and

cars. Like men do, like how relationships used to work, doctor.'

'And presumably by phone?'

'Yes, he was a bloody menace! Once he rang me thirteen times. He was a nightmare for calling!'

'Mr Stone, you know we have managed to retrieve all of your belongings now from the police, so we have your phone. Could you show me Robbie's number on there?'

Charlie paused.

'What is this, doc? Is he in trouble? You want me to stitch him up the way Trev stitched me? No way. And for the record, Trev was working. He was doing a job, he tricked me, he won and it's over. Let bygones be bygones.'

'I see, but-'

'He was just following orders, you know?'

'Yes, Mr-'

'-So just fucking leave it, all right! There's no need to get these lads in trouble for something that's done. Everyone's fucking lost out here. All of us.'

Charlie's monologue reached a crescendo. The dawning realisation hit him, not like a thunderbolt more like a wave, understanding seeped through his pores via osmosis.

'Mr Stone, can you show me...' the doctor realised he had won. Charlie was in check, pending mate. He had nowhere to run, the game was up.

He slowly reached for his phone that had been

carefully placed on the sideboard, next to his keys and wallet.

He opened it. No messages.

He went to his call log:

Maddie

Tara (3)

Maddie

Jackson

Jo

Jackson

Tara.

Fuck.

He quickly went to messages and then to WhatsApp. The same.

'You… you must have deleted all of it, to make some point. To trick me…'

The doctor shifted uncomfortably in his seat.

'No way!' Charlie tapped at the phone harder, before launching it across the room.

'The character Robbie you described in the East Kent Arms is not the same person others described him as, nor is he the same image as your Robbie when seen on CCTV. The man you visited the East Kent Arms with has not been seen since he went to the pub with you, last Sunday.'

'He came with me to the Thraxin site…'

'No, reports say that was one man there, unidentified…'

'But… the, uh… Wolfire! Ask Frank!'

'Frank's dead, I am afraid, Charlie.'

'What, why?'

'Just calm down, Mr Stone.'

'The gym, check the CCTV at the gym.'

'There was a report of an…incident at a well-to-do gym in Ashford. Police are looking into it, yet the report suggests, a fight between two individuals.'

'Yes, Robbie and the other guy!'

Dr Pathon looked at Charlie unconvinced.

'Robbie is big, right?'

'Yeah, like a bear…'

'And bald?'

'That's right.'

'Well, the description that has been released by the police, suggests a tall man, with an average build, mousey-brown hair, green eyes…'

A delicate silence came into the room and the doctor sat on the edge of the bed.

Charlie looked up at the ceiling.

Eventually, the doctor spoke.

'Mr Stone, I have to be totally honest with you. There is no record of Robbie Oliver having been with you since the evening you first met. I checked to see whether anyone had wiped the phone logs at your service provider, they haven't been touched.'

'Am I going mad?' Charlie uttered.

Did anyone meet Robbie? Charlie thought to himself.

'This has been quite a... revelation, Mr Stone. I am going to give you some time to rest.'

The doctor exited the room.

Charlie found it hard, so hard to differentiate between reality and fiction currently. His image of Robbie had been powerful, vivid, like reality. Driving fork lift trucks into buildings, being rescued from the Facility, being talked back from the water's edge... what was real and what wasn't?

The door opened once more and in came a nurse. Sadly, for Charlie, not the pretty one he liked.

'Time for a rest, I am afraid, Mr Stone.'

'But... I need to know...' Charlie trailed off.

The nurse injected Charlie with the old happy serum once more and he said goodbye, if only for a moment, to this confusing, cruel world.

Back in his office Doctor Pathon made a call to Tara to share with her the information he had just gleaned from Charlie. As next of kin, she had asked to be kept informed of his progress.

'I understand that this is upsetting...' he started.

'Like a split personality or something?' Tara said, eyes staring straight ahead.

'No... not a split personality. What I think has happened to Charlie is a rather severe case of "Polyvagal Syndrome."'

'Poly-who-gel?'

'Yes. Hear me out here.'

'The polyvagal theory discusses the role of the vagus nerve in emotion regulation, social connection and fear response. Ultimately it argues there are three modes in which a human being experiencing severe trauma, can operate: connection, fight or flight or total shutdown.

I theorise that what we see in Mr Stone is a creation of an alter-ego as a reaction to the trauma he faced. Having read his medical records and indeed, the newspapers, it is clear to see that in the space of about a year, a year and a half maybe, the man suffered extreme levels of suffering, of both a physical and mental nature. We are talking the temporary removal from his family home, estrangement from his daughter, kidnap, torture, the death of more than one friend, I mean he went through it-'

'-He did, but what about people who are subjected to war crimes or the victims of Nazi death camps? Do they not experience severe trauma too?' Tara asked.

'Good point. I guess there are a few things to discuss there. For instance, that is not happening to one solitary person, usually it is happening to a group, so those may have found solidarity in one another in the same boat. Also, with Mr Stone, I think he felt he had no other option but to keep fighting the crime, the brutality he witnessed. In short, he created this 'Robbie' character to deal with these growing issues. He met Robbie, fleetingly, and based his fictional character around the traits he saw in him.'

'Like a Batman to Bruce Wayne?' Tara asked.

'No, far more complex and subconscious than that. Mr Stone had no idea he was acting these two roles. He believed Robbie was a real person, he created a friend a) because he needed one, b) he knew he had to protect himself and others and to do that he would be suffering more, putting himself in deeply dangerous situations. His conscious mind told him no, to fly, but something within him knew he needed to continue, to stay and fight. That's where Robbie came in.'

'So, his behaviour is a mental thing? He's gone crazy?'

'Again, Miss…. Walker, it's not that simple. This is a complex analogy… a complex theory, I mean I may be wrong. Robbie may well have been present throughout the past few weeks. He may be the head of some criminal operation and he may have wiped all evidence of his recent existence from the planet. It's difficult to say. As a doctor, I tend to go with what is the most rational and likely solution. Did you ever meet 'Robbie'?' The doctor looked at Tara.

'He never mentioned him once.'

'So, this break up, Miss Walker, was it recent?' the doctor asked.

'Very. It can't be to do with me, this… *madness*…'

'Oh, no. I mean. I wasn't suggesting that. It's

just… he has suffered, this man.'

Tara exhaled deeply. 'Yes, doctor. We all have.'

'I have nothing further to report at this time. Do you have any questions?' The doctor said gently.

'No doctor, thank you for your call.'

With that the doctor left his office and headed back towards Charlie's room.

'Well I never,' the doctor stood open-mouthed.

The bed was empty and Charlie was nowhere to be seen.

37

Charlie was in a deep, drug-induced sleep. Something, however, was pulling him back to consciousness. Like a fly in his ear, a permanent, endless buzzing.

It was his phone. Charlie normally had all notifications off, for everything. The world could wait. It was better than a phone buzzing constantly to Charlie. But of course, someone had been on his phone, checking it, before it was handed back to him. Some London copper investigating... forgetting to put the bloody settings back to how they should have been.

As such, Charlie's slumber was woken by that infuriating buzz.

He could have left it. But then it was there, all bright, the screen luring him in, and it could have been anything.

He had been in a coma for a number of days, he had missed a lot.

Like getting dumped by his fiancée via his boss.

Secretly, Charlie hoped it was Tara. It wasn't. It was Troy. Troy Wood. He had given up calling and had left a text message.

Meet me at Folkestone Beach tonight. 6pm. Plenty of time from Ealing. Troy x

Folkestone Beach? Amateur! Charlie was a DFL'er, but at least he knew the lingo.

I will see you on Sunny Sands, Troy. Charlie thought to himself.

He checked the time, 5.43pm.

The train pulled out of Sandling. Two stops to go.

He had spent the journey in a daze. In fact, he felt so wired he entertained the fact that this was all just a simulation.

He had read about simulation theory.

He liked it.

Like nothing was really real. It was all part of a great big, virtual computer game. He thought back to the times he had been in fear for his life. When he was in a dungeon in Germany and he was locked in and gassed.

Did he even feel scared at the time?

He must have done.

When he was forced to torture teenage girls at the hand of Rosenkreutz' cult.

At the time he must have felt abhorred, nauseous. Now it seemed like an ethereal nightmare. It didn't matter. It was a moment in time that had gone.

Just like now.

What would occur would be immaterial.

Charlie could be captured or tortured.

He could be killed on the spot.

The world would keep turning and none of it would really make a great deal of difference.

Someone else would take his place as the hero

cop with emotional issues.

Someone else would use dark forces to gain and keep power.

Someone else would keep Tara warm at night.

Nothing mattered. Really.

It was good to be going back to the sea. The simulation sea, to swallow him up, swallow him whole.

To say goodbye.

The train pulled in to Folkestone Central. Charlie exited and began walking.

He tried to compute his feelings. His anger, rage and bile rose at the thought of Troy Wood and his activities.

But it didn't matter anymore.

Like Jackson said, if it wasn't Troy, it would be someone else.

The town centre was cold, grey and desolate. A living breathing 24/7 recession.

The old high street with its colour and vibrancy. It's renewed, independence and optimism.

The harbour with its hope.

And then Sunny Sands. Where it all began.

Charlie looked out over the mermaid statue, sitting proudly, and looked at the empty beach.

Empty that is apart from one man, sitting on the sand, looking out to sea.

Charlie looked at the walkway around the beach. There was no-one there.

Surely Troy had a gunman? Someone to take Charlie out if things got aggressive?

Maybe he was higher, atop the cliffs.

Maybe he wasn't.

Charlie walked down.

The hunched figure of Troy Wood didn't move, he just sat holding his knees. Hair blowing in the strong breeze. Charlie moved nearer.

Ethereal. Like a simulation. Like he was walking on air, like nothing really mattered.

He was standing next to his nemesis.

'Sit down, Charlie.'

Charlie sat on the sand.

The two men looked at each other.

'Hm. Your experiences have done you no favours, Charlie.' Troy said, a smile creeping across his face.

Charlie hadn't looked in a mirror. He dared not.

'I could say the same, Troy. Greying. Lines around the eyes.'

Troy nodded, smiled, looked away.

'It's been a terrifying time, since we last spoke in person. At the Best Western. Those years ago.'

'Terrifying? It seemed like a glorious rise through 'The Order,' straight to the top. No more the little man, eh Troy?'

'I can see how it looked. It wasn't like that. It wasn't what I wanted.'

'Oh, really?'

Troy turned to Charlie.

'Really.'

'So, what is this? Redemption? A public sorry and all is forgiven? Don't make me laugh.'

'I couldn't give two shits about your forgiveness, Charlie. We have both been through our own hell. Different versions. The same outcome. Two broken men.'

'Yes, but one was fighting the bad guy and one was the bad guy, Troy.'

'Is it that simple? Do you really believe, still, after all you have been through, that it is that simple?'

Charlie paused and thought about the question.

Was it that simple? The good wolf and the bad wolf? Or was it complex, nuanced, grey area'd? Were there always extenuating circumstances, reasons and excuses? Deadlines to miss, collateral damage?

'Yes. It is that simple.'

'Do you know, Charlie, the only reason you are alive is because I wanted you to be? I installed Trevor to find you, to lure you in, to keep you alive, you know that don't you?'

'What about 'The Carver?' Did you want him to keep me alive?'

'He has nothing to do with me...'

'Really? Come on, Troy. Don't take me for a fool.'

Troy looked at Charlie, his eyes told a different story, that he was in fact telling the truth.

'So, who was he to do with? Because he is a right bastard, you know?'

Troy sniggered. The guards were down briefly. Men were simple when you cut through the bravado and bullshit. A little quip, a shared experience, a connection is all it takes.

'Yes. That's a whole other story. I wanted to see you to tell you, I never wanted all of this to happen. Cliched though it may sound, there were levels to The Order, some that I was nowhere near. I was their poster boy, the one who rose through the ranks, the one who could keep you hanging on a line. Ultimately, the one who would take the fall. You understand?'

Charlie nodded.

'I wanted you alive because we were friends. I didn't want to harm you… not like that.'

'Are you serious? So, you have been kicked out of The Order, taken the fall for the real criminals behind closed doors, and you want everything you have done to be forgotten?'

'Nothing can ever be forgotten, Charlie. You know that as well as I do. But I do want an easy peace. A distant alliance. This ends here.'

Charlie looked out at the sea. The waves crashed menacingly, the sky grew dark overhead, the wind whipped sand over their hands, over their clothes.

'OK.'

'There is something else, Charlie.'

'Go on.'

'Tara. She's staying at my place in Sandgate.'

'That's funny.'

'It's a fact. She wants it done and over with you. I said I would speak to you.'

'*You* would speak to me?'

'Charlie, she wants security, she wants safety-'

'-And she will get that from you?'

'I've been set up by them. An allowance, I'll do well. Just got to keep my head down. Maybe write. I don't know yet.'

Charlie laughed.

'Yes, Troy. You have been a great friend.'

'Why don't you call her?' Troy said calmly.

Charlie took out his phone and rang her number. He waited for her to pick up. She always picked up, but this time it rang out. Charlie put the phone back in his pocket.

Troy picked up his own phone and rang Tara's number.

'Hey. Are you OK?' he said into the receiver.

Charlie could hear her voice on the line. His fiancée's. The mother of his child.

'Yes, on the beach. It's windy. OK, I'll call you in a bit.' Troy hung up. His point was made.

'You can be angry, Charlie. You can hit me. You can do what you like if it makes you feel better. But it needs to end here. Or it will kill us both. And I have had enough.'

Charlie looked at Troy. Troy stared back.

After a long wait, Charlie rubbing the sand deeper into the beach with his heels, spoke.

'I'll see you around, Troy.'

Charlie stared at him. Troy didn't know what to say. What he did know was that it was time for him to go. Time to leave.

Troy nodded, got up and walked away. Relieved, shocked that Charlie Stone didn't want vengeance, retribution.

Charlie lay back.

He felt deep-rooted pain, in his chest, in his heart. But anger had subsided.

This can't be a simulation. If it was, why would it hurt so much?

Charlie didn't know how long he laid on the sand, but when he opened his eyes, he looked directly at the stars.

He took his phone, wallet and keys from his pocket and placed them onto the sand.

He got up and walked towards the water's edge. At the shoreline, he took his shoes and socks off and continued walking into the water.

He looked out to sea, the dark abyss. The final reckoning. The easy option. Swallow him whole.

He closed his eyes and his legs moved, but not enough to take him further in. He was stuck in his tracks.

He looked out at the sea. He looked up at the stars then stepped back towards dry land.

'Time to feed the good wolf.'

EPILOGUE

Maddie drank her J20 in lightning quick speed. Kids. They never tell you they are thirsty. Always hungry. Charlie ordered another one, while taking a sip of his Heineken Zero.

There was a big event on at Junction 13. Summer had arrived, lockdown had been and gone. There was a band playing and a real buzz around Folkestone. The place was busy, and when it was, it became like a sweatbox. Punters leaned into the bar, waving notes at the staff. Everyone was in short sleeves, and the usual crowd were in. Jeff, Phil, a new guy called Leon, Sharn was behind the bar, rushed off her feet, but smiling.

'Did you know that when dinosaurs roamed the earth there were, like, thousands of them? All different types.' Maddie shouted over the reggae music that the band were playing.

'Oh yeah?'

'Yeah! A lot died out with disease, the slower ones got eaten...'

'How did they all become extinct in the end, Mad?'

'Meteor crashed into earth and wiped them all out.'

'Do you really believe that? I heard they all took up smoking and died from that.'

Maddie paused, then looked at Charlie and smiled.

'Don't be silly, dad!'

Jacko came in, only ten minutes late. He had both his children with him, Izzy and Bryce. The men hugged and Charlie ordered him a pint of Fosters.

'Everything OK?' Jacko asked.

The kids started chatting and Izzy got out a colouring book that her and Maddie pored over.

'Yeah, better,' Charlie said.

'Summer helps.'

'That it does.'

'How's everything?'

'Good. Very good…'

Jacko looked quizzically at his old friend.

'Well, better.' Charlie said sheepishly.

'And…Tara?'

'Yeah, fine. Fine. She never seems happy, but not my problem now.'

Jacko nodded. The men clinked their glasses to the summer in Folkestone.

As the day warmed up, the large glass windows of Junction 13 turned the interior into a greenhouse.

Jacko had to work in the morning, so he got a cab and took his children back home.

Charlie took Maddie over the road for an ice cream.

As the pair walked along the high street back towards Folkestone Central Station, the ice cream melted rapidly on Maddie's cone.

'Here, don't get stressed. Lick it quick!'

As Maddie moved her face down to it, the lump of ice cream fell from the cone onto the concrete and was promptly devoured by a pair of lurking seagulls.

'Dammit!' she said. Getting upset and a little angry.

'Calm down, Mad. It's OK.'

'But this stuff always happens to me!'

'It's just a bit of bad luck, relax! Let's go back and get another.'

As Maddie's rage abated, Charlie put his arm around his daughter.

'Have I ever told you about the story of the two wolves?'

'Probably, but go on anyway,' Maddie said in a monotone voice, still dejected by losing her ice cream.

'Well, an ancient proverb says there are two wolves inside of us. A good one and a bad one. If you feed the good one, it will grow stronger than the bad one and will win.'

'Hmm. A bit simple, dad. But I get it.'

'Well, I'm trying to feed the good wolf these days.'

'Is that why you are not working for the police anymore?'

'Correct.'

'Because it was dangerous and made you unhappy.'

Charlie looked surprised at his daughter's understanding.

'Yes, you're right. Yes. So, I'm keeping it simple now. Just, you and me against the world, eh?'

'That's all we need, dad,' Maddie said smiling at Charlie.

'Same again?'

'Yeah, but maybe get it in a tub, rather than a cone, this time.'

Charlie smiled, 'Good thinking.'

Maddie waited outside, as the shop was small and busy, while Charlie went and got another ice cream.

The shop owner gave it to him on the house, after his tale of seagull woe.

Charlie got outside and handed the ice cream over.

'You know, you will always have me dad, right?'

Charlie looked at Maddie and hugged her tight.

'I hope so, kiddo. I hope so.'

They hotfooted it to the train as Maddie wanted a Chinese take away, one of her dad's special pick n'mixes for dessert and West Ham were on. So, happy times.

As they crossed the zebra crossing, under the bridge by Folkestone Central, a shout came from across the street, behind them.

'Ere Charlie! How you doing, son?'

The voice was loud, brash and familiar. Robbie? It couldn't be?

'Char, wait up will ya?'

Charlie grabbed Maddie's arm and sped her up.

'Come on, I'll race you to the station!'

The ice cream tub fell from her hands as she sprinted as fast as she could up to the top of the ramp, narrowly beating her dad in a photo finish.

Charlie got the tickets and asked Maddie to keep going up towards the platform.

He followed swiftly after. The voice spoke again.

'Charlie? Why are you ignoring me, pal?'

Charlie stopped and turned.

'Because of the bloody good wolf all right?'

There was silence.

The electronic barriers to the station closed slowly behind Charlie, as he turned and walked with his daughter towards platform 1.

THE END

ACKNOWLEDGEMENTS

Thank you goes in no particular order to my wife Tnaesha Twohig who is my biggest fan and reads the book first and provides endless encouragement.

Her ideas and commitment to this project in particular, I am extremely grateful for. If I bring to Tnaesha a problem in the text that I can't solve, she can. That is invaluable, so thankyou, thankyou, thankyou.

Also to my Mum, Edwina Twohig, who casts a realistically critical eye and also for her support.

Skyla Twohig, my daughter who helps me believe that anything is possible and is the inspiration in a lot of these books.

Vicky Feaver for breathing new life into an old dog (wolf), 'Chelle Whitham for her enthusiasm and support, Kerry Barnes for her knowledge, help and support.

Finally, the people of Junction 13, which is now a beautiful moment in time, that we can never go back too. Hopefully some of the scenes in this book will bring back the memories, when they start to fade.

If you like this book, it is really important to me that you let me know via Amazon review, socials or tjtwohig1@yahoo.co.uk

If you didn't like this book, I'm sorry. You can let me know at the above email address.

www.trevortwohig.com

If you need any help or support on any of the issues raised in this novel, please use the following links.

Samaritans – 116 123
SANEline – 0300 304 7000
Strongline – 0800 915 0400

or visit

Mind.org
Fathers-4-justice.org

Printed in Great Britain
by Amazon

59051557R00184